Hoofbeats

Katie and the Mustang

Book Three

by KATHLEEN DUEY

DUTTON CHILDREN'S BOOKS
NEW YORK

Copyright © 2004 by Kathleen Duey

CIP Data is available.

Published simultaneously by Dutton Children's Books and Puffin Books,
divisions of Penguin Young Readers Group
345 Hudson Street, New York, New York 10014
www.penguin.com

Printed in USA · First Edition

10 9 8 7 6 5 4 3 2 1

ISBN 0-525-47274-6

My childhood memories are set to hoofbeats:
a fog-softened gallop on a lonely morning; the joyous
clatter of friends pounding down the Canal Road;
a measured, hollow clop of a miles-to-go July afternoon;
the snow-muffled hoofbeats of wintertime; the squelching
rhythm of a close race with a rainstorm. These books
are for my dear friends, the horses of my childhood—
Buck, Ginger, Steve, and Cherokee Star.

Thank you all.

CHAPTER ONE

❧ ❧ ❧

*The oxen walk slowly, with ropes and creaking
wood binding them to the great weight they pull for the
two-leggeds. The closeness of so many two-leggeds
makes me uneasy still. I am glad the little one keeps us
a small distance apart.*

That first morning was terrible—it took so long to leave Council Bluff that I had time to wonder if I was doing the right thing, going west by myself. Without Hiram and the wagon, I felt strange, like I was enclosed in lantern glass, somehow cut off from everyone else.

The Mustang was walking stiff-kneed, his head high and his nostrils flared. Holding the lead rope, walking him in circles to calm him, talking to him, kept me busy. He was a comfort in all the commotion.

Babies were crying, roosters crowing, dogs barking. And everyone was talking and shouting. The

Kyler girls were laughing, fidget-footed. Julia insisted on carrying around their white cat until Mrs. Kyler finally scolded her.

My blanket bundle, a little box of my spare clothes, and 150 pounds of the bacon Hiram had bought was in Mr. and Mrs. Kyler's wagon. I kept wishing I could catch a glimpse of my gray blanket through the puckered-cloth opening. It felt wrong to have my mother's book and my father's silver shoe buckles in someone else's wagon.

In front of us were families I had never met—people who had signed up with Mr. Teal long before the Kylers had. As the dust thickened from the milling hooves, I saw the shapes of skulking boys in the gray dawn light, doing nothing to help that I could see. They were barefoot like me, like most of the children.

Every five or ten minutes, the Mustang jerked his head up and bugled a loud, high-pitched whinny. Half the mares in the Kylers' band answered him. I was sure that Delia's and Midnight's voices were among the chorus, but I couldn't tell. The Mustang could. He quieted. He tolerated being away from the mares, but he still wanted to know he had a friend nearby.

Poor Mr. and Mrs. Kyler looked stubborn and sad. I could only imagine how they felt. It was hard on them to leave Annie behind, her hands wrapped in bandages, in so much pain. It was a terrible decision, and we all knew what it meant. They would most likely never see their daughter again. They couldn't even stay for the wedding. We had all heard stories of how a day or two at journey's end made the difference between life and death.

We were the second wagon train forming up. The first was Mormon folks. I remembered Hiram saying they'd had trouble back where they were from. Whatever it was, it must have made them stop trusting strangers. They kept to themselves.

Blinking, my eyes stinging from the dust, I walked the Mustang out to one side of the line of wagons. There were nineteen wagons ahead of us that I could see. Most were prairie schooners like the Kylers had; a few were farm wagons.

Mr. Teal had started down the line, shouting advice about harness adjustments and water barrel strapping and a lot more that I couldn't make out.

The Kyler girls were standing in a group now, bunched up behind their grandparents' wagon, holding still for once. I counted. There were five girls. Julia with her long, dark braids and Polly, tall and thin—then the three younger girls, Mary May, Patience, and Hope. I wasn't sure which was which of the little girls. They were holding hands, watching Mr. Teal come closer.

"Keep a distance between the wagons," Mr. Teal was shouting. "Watch your children. Teach them to walk off to the side, to stay away from the wagon wheels…children have been killed."

Julia and Polly pulled the little girls off to the side opposite mine. The dust made it nearly impossible for me to see them, even though they had moved less than twenty feet farther from me.

"Some are asking about the war with Mexico," Mr. Teal shouted. "Word is that it has begun. We won't be crossing anywhere near the trouble, so there's nothing to fear."

Mr. Teal walked a few more wagons down the line and started over, repeating the same things. For another half hour or more, the wagons all stayed put, the men milling around and shouting, getting people and supplies sorted out. It took a long time to get gathered up behind the party of Mormon folks who were moving out ahead of us.

Mr. Teal wanted the wagons in a certain order. The Kylers argued not to be split up. Mr. Teal agreed to that much, but he wanted a party of all men at the rear of the train instead of Andrew and Hannah Kyler and their baby.

"They got thirty head of horses running along-side. We'll choke on the dust," one of the men argued. He was a tall man and had a beard as thick as dog's fur. "They joined a good week after us," he added, then spat. "It ain't fair."

"We aren't looking to cause any trouble," Andrew Kyler said.

"It's a simple matter of defense, Mr. Silas," Mr. Teal said, finally raising his voice. "If we hit trouble, four armed men will be better placed at the end than a couple with an unweaned child."

Mr. Teal's face darkened when Mr. Silas shot back an angry protest. "Hear me well," Mr. Teal said evenly. "I won't abide a man who argues away precious time on the first morning. A wagon train has to work like a family or too many of us won't get to Oregon at all."

The tall man nodded reluctantly. "For now, then.

But we ain't staying back there the whole way."

Mr. Teal acted like he hadn't heard. "We'll see Indians by and by," he said, turning to face the crowd that had gathered. "I don't like them to think we can't protect ourselves. Most seem as honest as daylight, but we don't understand them or their ways yet, and I like to be careful."

In order to line up, we had to circle a quarter mile down the valley, turning in a tight curve to come back. Following the wagons, I got a look at the bleak little tents and shacks the Mormon folks had wintered in.

There were a number of men in their line with high-wheeled carts like miniature wagons without mules or oxen hitched to them. They had no setup for harnesses, no singletrees or wagon tongues at all. They were built with U-shaped push bars. These were fastened to the sides of the little wagons and extended far enough frontward so a man could walk inside the U shape. The men pushed the carts by gripping the bar and shoving them along.

The Mormon folks seemed much better organized than the rest of us. We could hear them singing as they started out. I admired that. I sure didn't feel like singing. I was scared.

Once we came back around, the wagons falling into the order that Mr. Teal wanted them, we just kept going. When I realized he wasn't going to stop us again, I turned and ran a little way back, the Mustang trotting to keep up with me. "Thank you, Hiram," I called. "Good-bye, Annie!"

They both waved, and I could tell that Annie was crying. I felt so sorry for her. In a few minutes at most, she would get her last glimpse of her family as we strung out behind the last of the Mormon families, all of us headed up and over the bluffs that framed the wide, brown Missouri River.

As the plodding oxen pulled the wagons up the first gentle rise, the Kylers kept shouting to Annie, all of them, grinning and waving, wiping at their eyes. The girls jumped up and down, waving their arms. Annie's brothers called out final farewells and wedding blessings.

My throat ached with sadness for them, and a bitter envy I would never admit to anyone. I led the Mustang along a little faster as the road got steeper and did not look back again. I imagined that my parents and sister were in one of the wagons. If it hadn't been for the fever, it might have come true. My father had talked about it off and on.

My mother would have done fine on the trail. She was brave and strong, and she would have been singing hymns along with the Mormon women. Mary Kyler would have loved her.

"My uncle Jack will never believe I've come all the way by myself," I told the Mustang, trying to calm myself. I was feeling shivery and scared. The Mustang lowered his head to touch my shoulder with his muzzle. Then he tossed his mane and whinnied once, loud and long. The mares answered him.

"You all right, Katie?" Mrs. Kyler called to me.

I looked at her tearstained face and nodded, a big exaggerated motion so she could see it through the dust. She was such a nice woman, asking after me when she was the one leaving a daughter behind. I *was* fine, I told myself. I was on my way to find my family, and I couldn't wait to get there.

CHAPTER TWO

۩ ۩ ۩

*Herds of two-leggeds take a long time to choose
a direction and begin to travel. But once they start, they
keep on, all day, strung out over the land. The little one
has learned to find good grass, and I am grateful.*

$\mathcal{T}$he road was steep and narrow going over
the bluff, but once we topped it, the horizons
were so wide, so glorious, that I heard a spontane-
ous cheer rise along the line of wagons.

"Oregon ho!" Mr. Teal shouted at the top of
his lungs, and the cheer swelled. A few of the men
tossed their hats high.

Mr. Kyler was straight as a ramrod on the driver's bench. Mrs. Kyler was twisted around, still
looking back toward Annie and Hiram even though
she couldn't see them anymore.

Andrew Kyler was herding his stock along on the other side of the wagons, almost even with Mr. Silas. I didn't want to get too close to the mares, or they would try to follow the Mustang. And I didn't want to be close if the men started arguing.

I walked fast, then broke into a running stride for a little ways, passing wagons, each with its hitch of oxen plodding in pairs under their heavy wooden yokes. The wagon train was much longer now that the wagons were spread out.

The Kyler girls were walking between the tailgate of Ralph and Ellen Kyler's wagon and the team of oxen that pulled their grandparents' wagon— still off to one side like Mr. Teal had told them. For once, they were subdued and quiet.

I kept walking fast until I was ahead of them, then I slowed and glanced back. They were whispering to one another now, their heads close together.

A little girl with ashy blonde hair pulled one of Julia's braids. "Hope!" Julia said sharply, jerking her hair free.

Well. Great day in the morning. After all this time, I knew which one was Hope. Did any of them know my name? If they did, they never used it.

The Mustang broke into a prancing trot, blowing out whooshing breaths, his neck arched. I ran a little to keep up with him, then gradually pulled on the lead, bringing him back to a walk. His ears were pricked straight forward, and his tail streamed out behind him.

"It's all the open sky, isn't it?" I asked him. He nosed at my shoulder, then lifted his head and pranced another few strides before he settled.

I glanced back at the girls and saw Polly staring at me. I looked aside quickly, then realized she was probably looking at the Mustang. He looked beautiful in the early sunlight, his mane and tail fanned out in the breeze.

I looked away. I didn't want the girls crowding around the Mustang anytime, but especially not when he was already in high spirits and a little nervous. The last thing I needed was for some giggling girl to spook him and get herself kicked. I shivered, thinking about it, and led the Mustang a little farther away from the long line of wagons. I had to be careful.

"You're calmer than you were," I told him. "But Hiram was right. No one will ever mistake you for a farm horse." It was true. When something startled him, his instinct was to fight.

I walked a little faster, and the Mustang kept up without my tugging on the rope at all. I slowed as I came up even with the last of the Kylers' wagons. The driver was one of their sons, I knew that much, and that his name was Charles. His wife was tiny, almost child-sized. They both looked young. I wondered which of the girls belonged to them. They both waved at me, and I waved back.

Then I walked a little faster, keeping my eyes on the road ahead, until I was more or less abreast with the next wagon—a couple I had never met. The man and his wife smiled at me. I nodded and smiled at them.

The Mustang arched his neck and stepped lightly. "Are you trying to impress their mules?" I teased him quietly. The man was driving a span of six mules, big reddish ones—a color I had never seen before. He and his wife were both heavyset, rosy-faced people. They smiled at me again, and I smiled back, then looked away, a little uneasy.

There were so many strangers. Most of the Kylers were strangers to me, really. The Mustang was walking close behind me, and he chose that moment to touch my shoulder with his muzzle, his breath warm on my neck in the chilly morning air. I patted him, grateful for his friendship.

I heard the sound of girlish laughter behind us and refused to turn and look. The Kyler girls. I heard them talking, then another burst of laughter, and I glanced back in spite of myself. "You can't do it that way!" Polly exclaimed. "You have to guess, then it's Mary May's turn." I saw her lower her head, talking earnestly. It sounded like some kind of guessing game.

"I'll probably get to know the Kyler girls better now," I whispered to the Mustang. "Whether I want to or not. I'll have to shelter in their grandparents' wagon when the weather gets bad."

I longed for Hiram and our little wagon and turned to look back toward Council Bluff. It had disappeared. Even Kanesville was impossible to see from here. The land was so level on either side of the steep-sided valley that it was completely hidden, the edges of the bluffs blending with distance as though nothing lay between them at all.

I turned back and saw a little boy peeking out of

the back of the covered wagon in front of me. "Oregon ho!" he shouted at me. He looked so merry that I couldn't help but smile at him. "Oregooooon ho!" he shouted a second time.

There was a little rill of laughter among the adults who were close enough to hear. He shouted a third time, and his father glanced around and saw me staring. He grinned. "Morning!" he called. "You've met our son, Toby. We're the McMahons."

"How do you do?" I answered him politely. I found myself angling the Mustang closer so he wouldn't have to shout.

"Doing fine, this morning," he said. "We were about to die of waiting back in Kanesville. We'd been there—"

"Nearly two weeks," Mrs. McMahon said.

"The man we signed on with had to go back east," Mr. McMahon said. "So we had to look for another guide but—"

"The best of them had more folks than they wanted for their parties," his wife said.

I smiled. It was like talking to the same person, divided over two bodies. One started the sentences, and the other finished them.

"That's a handsome animal," Mrs. McMahon said, pointing at the Mustang.

"We were wondering earlier—" Mr. McMahon began.

"Where'd you get an animal like that?" Mrs. McMahon asked.

"He's from the Oregon country somewhere," I said, hoping they wouldn't ask me any more. The gathered iris of osnaburg canvas behind them parted, and Toby was suddenly climbing onto the driver's bench from the back. He scooted down, positioning himself between his parents like a hen settling into straw.

I smiled and waved at him, but then I dropped back a little. "Sometimes I wish you were plain as a mud hen," I told the Mustang. "You always draw a question or two."

He shook his mane, probably to chase off a fly, but I laughed. It looked as though he had meant to argue with me. "Oh, I know. If you were less handsome, Midnight and Delia wouldn't answer every time you neighed at them, would they?" I tapped his shoulder and he danced away from me, then sidled closer again. I laughed aloud.

Then I noticed that the Kyler girls were all look-ing at me. Polly waved and I waved back, but then I blushed and lowered my eyes. I faced straight ahead for a while, feeling silly. Why should I care if the Kyler girls thought I was odd, talking to a horse? But I did. I did.

The rutted road lay before us, disappearing in the distance. The sky was wide and light blue with only a few clouds visible to the north. The ground beneath my feet was smooth and soft—and chilly from the cold night.

The sun would soon warm it, I was sure. It felt good to be up out of the valley and on the high ground. I could see all the way to forever in all four directions.

I leaned close to the Mustang's ear and whis-pered so low that the Kyler girls wouldn't know I was talking to him again.

"Oregon!" I breathed. "We're on our way."

CHAPTER THREE

❧ ❧ ❧

*It is so good to be away from the tangle of scents in
the valley. Here, when I am upwind of the two-leggeds,
I am content to walk with the little one, listening to
her make her soft sounds.*

I t took almost two hours to get the wagons in
a circle that first night. The drivers had botched
it at our supper stop, and Mr. Teal was determined
to get it done proper for the night. It sounds like a
simple thing to do, but it isn't.

If one of the wagons is angled wrong, the next
one can't be placed right; then instead of a circle,
it winds up looking like a misshapen egg with gaps
between the wagons wide enough for any horse or
ox to waltz right through.

Mr. Teal made everyone start over three times, getting all the wagons back into a long line, then filing off in a curve. I walked the Mustang off to one side and let him graze while the men were popping their whips and shouting at the oxen.

They came around one last time. The oxen were bawling with hunger by the time we finally got it done. The sun had almost gone down before anyone had the harnesses off their working stock.

"Tomorrow we will be stopping earlier," Mr. Teal shouted, standing on the McMahons' driver's bench. "You need practice, but it'll get easier."

"Amen to that," someone answered, and everyone laughed.

I kept the Mustang grazing until people had their campfires lit and their suppers started. Then, when things had quieted down, I led him back to the ring of wagons and guided him over Mr. and Mrs. Kyler's wagon tongue.

He lifted his front hooves high and hopped his back ones over the long oak pole that served as the anchor for all the harness straps. He was whinnying back and forth with Delia and Midnight the whole time we walked toward them.

"Good thing no one else has a stallion," Andrew Kyler said, watching the Mustang nudge the two mares to the edge of the herd. The horses and oxen would have the inside of the circle grazed flat by morning, and I was glad the Mustang had already gotten his fill.

"Here, Katie," Mrs. Kyler said, patting the ground beside her when I got back to her wagon. "Will you stir this while I get the biscuits?"

I knelt beside the fire and smelled salt pork and beans heating in the pot—leftovers from last night's supper.

I dragged the long-handled ladle through the big pot, making sure the beans weren't sticking to the cast iron and burning. Nothing tasted worse than burnt beans, and I didn't want to be the one responsible for ruining everyone's meal.

I heard Mrs. Kyler banging around in the jockey box that was mounted on the side of their wagon. Hiram and I had packed our kitchen goods inside our little farm wagon, but it was much harder to pack and unpack one of these high, covered freight wagons. Most of the women kept their kitchens in the wooden boxes.

"There it is!" Mrs. Kyler said, holding up a slotted spoon. "This lets the water run out when I serve up the plates. Two of my boys hate sloppy beans."

I stirred, watching her work, admiring the everyday grace in her worn, stained hands. She tore thick handfuls of grass and laid it flat to get it out of her way and to make a clean place to set her tins and utensils. She spread a cloth and set a butter crock on it, then glanced up at me.

"Melted from the sun, and it'll be rancid in two days, but I traded for it in Kanesville—thought it'd be a nice surprise tonight." She pushed back the cloth on the biscuit box and stood up, pressing her hands against the small of her back. "All leftovers. Supper's simple to fix tonight." She stood looking upward at the darkening sky, stretching, then leaned over and slipped her pot stick through the arch of the bale, and lifted the heavy pot off the fire.

"Come and get supper!" she shouted, skimming the side of the pot with the ladle three or four times before she started dishing up the food.

In minutes, I was surrounded by Kylers. I took my plate and backed away, finding a spot beside one of the wagon wheels where I could lean back a little and eat in comfort. The beans tasted good. Anything tastes good when you are hungry enough, but Mrs. Kyler did make good beans—not too salty. She must have washed some of the salt out of the bacon before she cut it up.

"How are your feet?"

I looked up, startled to see Julia standing over me. "Fine."

"They aren't sore?" she asked. "Mine are bruised all over."

I shook my head. "I walked most the way from Scott County barefoot."

"Julia!" one of the girls called. I looked past Julia and saw Polly and Hope. They were standing with two other girls I didn't know. They weren't Kylers. I had never seen them before.

"Julia!" Polly called again. "What are you doing? Come on!"

Julia shook her head. "She's bossy. She's the oldest cousin, so she thinks she can tell the rest of us what to do."

I nodded like I understood perfectly, but the truth was, I didn't. If I had any cousins, they were in Oregon, and I had never met them. I didn't know whether they were boys or girls.

Polly started off, then glanced back at me. For an instant, I thought she might ask me to come with her, but she didn't. I felt a little stab of disappointment, but I knew it was silly. I had to help out. I had to earn my way with the Kylers. I didn't want to be beholden to them for anything if I could help it.

I finished my food, then went and checked on the Mustang while Mr. Kyler and his sons ate their seconds. They all laughed and joked as they ate, comparing complaints and worries, teasing one another.

I helped clean the plates. It wasn't hard. Everyone had been hungry enough to practically lick the tins clean. Mrs. Kyler showed me a trick—a way to twist a hank of grass into a pot scrub. We used as little water as we possibly could, washing the tins in a shallow tin basin, one after the other. When the plates were done, Mrs. Kyler restacked everything in the jockey box and closed the heavy lid.

Then she sighed and came back to the fire. "I think we can leave what's left in the pot beside the fire until morning," she said, pushing her hair back from her forehead. "There's two wagons with dogs, but Mr. Teal said they had to be tied up at night."

"I didn't see any dogs," I told her.

She yawned. "Nor did I, but Mr. Teal said there were a couple."

"Thanks very much for supper, ma'am," I said, suddenly remembering my manners.

Mrs. Kyler reached out and stroked my hair. "Where do you want to sleep, Katie?"

I hadn't thought about it, and I didn't know what to say. I was used to sleeping beneath the wagon, so that's what I finally told her.

"Not inside?"

I shook my head.

"Julia sometimes sleeps with us, but she isn't going to tonight," Mrs. Kyler said. "Her mother wants her close."

I shook my head again.

"It's a fea-ther bed," Mrs. Kyler said in a sing-song voice. "A feather bed with a real bolster pil-loooow..." She was smiling.

A real bed. I hadn't slept in a real bed since home...you couldn't really call a pallet in a pantry a real bed. My mother had had a feather bed. In the winter, we had all slept in it to keep warm.

My eyes flooded with tears, and I turned away. "May I just sleep outside, ma'am?" I asked as evenly as I could.

Mrs. Kyler put her hand on my shoulder. "Of course."

She walked away, and I heard the wagon creak as she climbed up the steps at the rear gate. I spread my bedding and then went to check on the Mustang once more before I lay down. The mares were asleep. The Mustang was wide awake, his ears swiveling to catch every sound. He seemed calm enough and let me kiss his forehead.

Walking back to the Kylers' wagon, I could hear men's voices on the other side of the wide circle. I saw one campfire, built up and burning bright. Ten or fifteen men were standing around it, talking. Their voices sounded angry.

Lying beneath the Kylers' wagon, listening, I remembered what Mr. Teal had said. The wagon party had to become like a family, or fewer people would make it all the way to Oregon.

CHAPTER FOUR

✤ ✤ ✤

*I must never sleep for long. The mares depend on me to
hear a wolf, to scent distant fires—to know about
danger before it comes. It is hard, the two-leggeds
don't stop to doze mid-day. I am weary.*

*L*ate the next morning we came over a little
rise and saw the Elkhorn River. The men had
all been talking about it at breakfast. It wasn't wide,
or all that deep, they said, unless there had been
rain upstream. What they hadn't said was that the
Elkhorn was as curved as a snake's track in summer dust.

The Mustang had smelled the water a mile away,
I was sure. All of a sudden, he had tossed his head,
his nostrils flaring as he scented the breeze coming
toward us. Then he had picked up the pace, pulling

me along, outpacing the oxen easily. The road passed farmhouses and fields, and I wondered about the people who lived there, if the wagons passing made them want to go west or if the constant dust just made them angry.

The McMahons waved at me when I came up even with them. I smiled at little Toby; he was peeking out the back of the wagon again. Then I angled away from the wagons to keep clear of the other families and their children. The Mustang was prancing, pulling me along by the time we started downhill.

The wagons followed the rutted road with slow deliberation, Mr. Teal in the lead as he usually was, the big wagons swaying and creaking over every little bump. This slope was long and gradual, not like the steep descent into Council Bluff.

We crossed a path that had been worn by cattle; there were thousands of cloven hoofprints in the dirt. The farmers here let their cows run loose to graze, it looked like, and they had trampled a path down to the river. It was narrow and curved in long arcs, switching back and forth, always headed downhill, always within sight of the road—so I took it to escape some of the dust from the wagons.

I kept glancing at Mr. Teal, thinking he might call me back into the line, but he didn't seem to notice or care if I took a different route, so I kept going.

At first the path led us away from the wagons, then zigzagged back toward them. After the turn, I could see our whole party strung out in a long line. I pulled the Mustang to a halt and watched.

The wagons looked so different like this, from a distance. All the sounds were muted; I couldn't hear the voices, the wood axles creaking, the labored breathing of the oxen. I could just barely hear a dog barking. I spotted it, standing on the driver's bench, a big black dog with its legs splayed to keep its balance. I hadn't seen it before.

I hadn't seen a lot of things, I realized. There were four teams of mules—the rest were six- and eight-oxen hitches. One wagon had what looked like a birdcage hanging on the back gate. I saw three boys running in circles near the front of the party, their bare feet raising dust.

The drivers were all sitting easy, both hands loose on the reins. The sheer weight of the oxen— and their refusal to move forward any faster than

ↂ 27 ↂ

their usual plodding walk—was brake enough on this gentle decline.

The Mustang nudged my shoulder and shook his mane. I patted him, and he angled his body sideways, tugging at the lead rope, lowering his head to paw at the earth.

"All right," I told him. "But I can't go as fast as you can." So we went on with the Mustang holding his head so high that I could feel his breath on top of my head all the way down to the bottom. I hurried, afraid he would step on my heels if I didn't go fast enough.

The bottomlands were lined with cottonwood trees, and, as we got closer, I could see the Mormon party lined up beneath them. About half their wagons had gone across; fifteen or twenty were waiting.

Mr. Teal saw them about the same time I did. He shouted and stood in his stirrups, motioning to the first wagon to follow him—so of course, the whole line did, out into a meadow a half mile above the fording place.

I followed along, not in line, but traveling a parallel course across the wide, flat bottomland, walking beside the river. The grass was high in places where the cows hadn't gone much. The Mustang slowed down to grab mouthfuls of it as he walked. He kept on toward the water, though, and I didn't try to stop him. There was at least a half hour to wait before the other party was out of our way, and so long as I kept an eye on the wagons, there was no reason to go stand in the sun with everyone else.

The shade beneath the cottonwoods was deep and cool, and the Mustang drank from the shallows. I could see glimpses of the wagons crossing at the ford downstream. I was relieved to see people leading stock across. The river didn't look more than knee deep on the men.

I dipped one foot in the water, then the other. It was chilly, and it felt wonderful. I remembered Hiram's promise to teach me to swim. Now I might never learn.

I tangled my hands in the Mustang's mane. "I miss Hiram," I told him. "I know he loves Annie. I know he has every right to decide to get married, but I miss him."

A burst of derisive laughter made me spin around. A boy wearing a broad-brimmed hat was standing a little distance off, staring at me, his head tipped to one side and his face twisted into a mocking grin. "I never heard anyone talk to a horse like that in my whole life," he said.

I blushed and tried to think of something clever to say back to him, but I couldn't. He was standing in dappled sunlight, and I couldn't make out his features. I wasn't sure if he was one of the boys from our wagon party or not. I hoped not.

He lowered his voice. "Your horse ever talk back?" He laughed again, like he had just heard the funniest joke in the world.

"You live around here?" I asked, tightening my grip on the Mustang's lead rope. "Or are you going west?" I hoped he would answer without taunting me, that he'd stop being mean, but he didn't.

"Oh, it's best you don't talk to me," he said in a low voice, like he was being serious all of a sudden. "Your horse'll get jealous," he whispered.

He laughed again, then turned to leave, and the sun caught the side of his face. I could see blond hair sticking out from under the hat. He looked familiar in a vague way—maybe I had seen him in Council Bluff?

He ignored me completely, stopping to roll up

his trousers, wading into the shallows. He went on downstream, not looking back even once, skipping rocks on the surface of the water.

I waited until he was out of sight, then I hitched up my skirts and let out the Mustang's lead rope so that he could keep grazing as I waded in up to my knees. The water was breathtakingly cool. The Mustang lifted his head and watched me, then waded in.

I cupped my hands and scooped up some water to drizzle over his face. He snorted, shaking his mane, then pawed at the water, soaking his own belly and drenching me. It made me laugh, and I found myself forgetting about the boy's mean jokes.

The sunlight flickered when a breeze swayed the canopy of cottonwood boughs overhead. The Mustang pranced along, sloshing through the shallows. He pawed at the water again, and I splashed him back. Then I ran and he trotted behind me. He stopped abruptly when he noticed a patch of grass on the bank—like a child who notices candy on a table he is running past. It made me laugh again. My voice sounded too high, too squeaky—*unfamiliar.* How long had it been since I had heard myself laughing?

I finally waded out, and the Mustang followed,

his legs and tail streaming water. As we came out of the trees I saw that Mr. Teal had taken this opportunity to give the drivers a practice session at circling the wagons. It had gone better this time than it had the night before, but the circle still wasn't exactly round.

I could see Mr. Teal standing with four or five men, all talking more or less at once. One of the men was Mr. Silas. As I got closer, it sounded like he was still complaining about having to be last in line.

It was clear that Mr. Silas wasn't going to accept the position he had been asked to take. It was equally clear that Mr. Teal was irritated that the man wouldn't cooperate. I remembered his saying that a man who argued on the first day might not be welcome on the journey. What about a man who argued on the first day *and* the second day?

I stopped and let the Mustang graze. The Kylers waved at me, and I waved back to let them know I was watching and would be ready when the party headed toward the ford.

The Mustang was still eating eagerly, chewing steadily, when I heard Mr. Teal shout for the drivers to get ready. A few minutes later, he lifted one fist in the air, giving his usual yell of "Wagons ho!" as he led the way toward the ford. I stood still as the wagons got moving, the line forming again as each driver came out of the circle.

"Katie!" Mr. Kyler shouted at me. He was waving me closer. I led the Mustang toward him.

"Yes, sir?" I called back.

"You want Andrew to run the Mustang across with the rest of the herd? You can ride with us."

I shook my head before he finished talking. I was sure that Andrew Kyler knew a lot about farm horses and saddle horses, but the Mustang wasn't like any of them. He was awake and alert every minute, listening, scenting the air, watching everything. If something startled him and Andrew tried to drive him back into the herd, his drover's whip popping, the Mustang might try to fight.

"I'll come across with him," I called back. "I can lead him just fine."

It was too hard to explain anything at a shout. I had never told anyone that the Mustang had run away from me once, and then galloped back again. He might not come back the next time. I patted his neck to keep him standing steady and still. I didn't want Mr. Kyler to think he was skittish.

"He'd be fine with the herd," Mr. Kyler called back to me. "Teal looked. He says the ford is wide and shallow."

"It is," I called back. "I watched people crossing on foot. It's best if I just lead him across."

He shrugged and faced front—the McMahons' wagon was starting to move.

"Be careful," Mrs. Kyler called, leaning forward so I could see her.

"I will," I shouted back as their oxen began to move. As the wagon turned, I saw Polly looking out the back of the wagon. She didn't so much as smile at me. If she was riding with her grandparents, Julia was probably in the wagon, too. Maybe the younger girls were there as well.

I was glad I had insisted on leading the Mustang across myself. I would feel very out of place in the wagon with the Kyler cousins.

Through the spaces between the wagons, I saw other people leading stock along. One woman had a milk cow; an older man had a mare with a spindly legged foal. Mr. Teal galloped down the line, shouting instructions I couldn't hear, then circled his horse between two wagons to gallop toward me.

"Here we go!" someone shouted.

Mr. Kyler was popping the whip over the oxen's backs, and the wagon began to roll just as Mr. Teal got close enough to shout. "Wait until they are all across, you hear me?"

I nodded, and he spurred his horse around, galloping until he was back at the head of the line.

I led the Mustang off to the side to be out of the way, but I took him back toward the river so we could watch. Mr. Teal was shouting at the drivers as they passed, reminding them all not to start across until the team ahead of them was on the far bank.

The woman with the milk cow came to stand near me and introduced herself as Mrs. Craggett. "He tell you to wait until they were all across?"

I nodded. "It's probably safest."

She smiled. "I am sure you're right, but I also think that man just likes to shout orders."

I couldn't agree out loud; my mother had taught me never to criticize my elders. But in my heart, as I watched Mr. Teal galloping, pivoting his horse, making sure he had something to say to every single driver, I began to see what she meant.

As the ninth or tenth wagon came into position, I spotted the boy who had teased me. He was still wearing the odd hat. I stared, tangling my hand in the Mustang's mane without realizing I was doing it until my fingers got caught and I had to pull them free. The boy had his hat pulled low, and I couldn't really see his face, but it didn't matter. I recognized him anyway.

He was walking behind his parents' wagon, shoulders squared, tossing a rock up into the air, then catching it again, in rhythm with his steps.

My heart constricted. I was sure, even though I wasn't close enough to really see his face. It was the boy from Des Moines who had thrown a fist-sized rock at the Mustang. I was sure he had recognized me—he would remember the Mustang—when he had talked to me by the river.

"Something wrong, honey?" the woman with the cow asked me.

I shook my head. There was no point in telling her. There was nothing she could do. "I don't think so," I answered, and could only hope that it was true, that he wasn't as mean as he had seemed that day in Des Moines, that he would only tease and taunt me, not try to hurt the Mustang again.

When all the wagons were finally up on the other side, I led the Mustang across the river. Three or four men had stayed back, watching in case anyone needed help. I soaked my skirt, but I wasn't in any danger, not even for an instant.

The woman with the cow came over after me. The poor milker bawled all the way across the river, the cool water unpleasant on her udder and belly. The foal and mare made it fine.

On the far side of the river, I kept my eyes moving, scanning the trees and the sandy bank, but the boy wasn't around. I hung back, walking a little way behind the last wagon for the rest of the day.

CHAPTER FIVE

🐚 🐚 🐚

This seems a good place to me. A herd of horses
could live well here. But the little one and the rest of the
two-leggeds are going on. Perhaps they are looking
for forests and swifter, colder rivers. Maybe they are
going to the country I was born in.

$\mathcal{F}$rom the Elkhorn crossing, we went west,
then northwest, following the Platte River. The
road became ten roads, then twenty paths.

We crossed a dozen rivers that no one had names
for in the weeks that followed. Every river was scary
in its own way. Some were deep, some swift, some
were both.

Twice the men caulked the wagon beds and the
wagons were floated across, like clumsy boats, pulled
by ropes and teams of oxen on the shore. More
often, we drove across, the oxen hitched and

swimming. We always used a tow rope upstream and a fixed rope on the downstream side, to give anyone thrown into the water a chance to catch on and stay afloat.

Andrew lost one gelding, and the black dog was washed downstream in a current so swift that he was there one instant and lost in white foam and roaring water the next. The young man who had brought him whistled and called for days, every time we stopped, hoping that the dog had made it out of the river and was following, but he never came back.

There were dozens of streams and creeks, too. Most of them had no names that anyone of us knew, anyway. All the big rivers were scary, but no one drowned. We were lucky; we all heard many terrible stories of drownings from other travelers.

Mr. Barrett, the man who Mr. Stevens had planned to travel with, had talked about the Oregon trail, but we began to realize that there wasn't a single trail, not really—and that not all the rutted paths were good roads. The lay of the land mattered more than anything else. Sometime the best-worn paths led to marshes or creeks that had to be crossed—or couldn't be crossed—because of early rains.

Mr. Teal rode out every evening, scouting for the next day, but he couldn't always go far enough before dark to tell which was the best path to follow. He made his best guess, and we followed his advice. Mostly, he was right.

As we went, our days took on a pattern. We rose before it was light and fell to our chores, everyone stretching and yawning as they began their daily work. I would run to make sure the Mustang was all right, then hurry back to the Kylers' camp, shivering and hungry. It seemed like I was always hungry.

My first morning chore was to rake back the white ash, baring the still-hot coals that had lasted the night. Using twists of dry grass or dead twigs or whatever I had managed to gather the day before, I got the fire going again so Mrs. Kyler could start cooking breakfast.

I really liked this still-dark part of our days. We usually talked a little, shivering in the dawn dusk, keeping our voices down so that anyone trying to get a few extra minutes' sleep could do so.

I kept the fire very small, adding as little wood as I could and still keep it burning while Mrs. Kyler heated coffee and cooked eggs or ham. She was quick. She wasted no time at all getting started on breakfast in the morning. Half the time she had the skillet ready before I had rekindled the fire. I appreciated it. We had to be very careful of firewood. It was hard to find.

There weren't many cottonwood trees—they only grew along the creeks and rivers. And even when we saw a lot of trees in a day, there wasn't much deadwood in easy reach. The easy pickings had been taken by people who came before us.

It was my job to keep us in wood since I could range around—and make my way into thick copses of trees the wagons had to avoid. I brought back all I could carry, and put it in an old wire hayrick Mr. Kyler had fastened onto the back of the wagon. Julia, Polly, and Hope had the same job, but they rarely found as much wood as I did—all three of them put together. They weren't spoiled exactly, and they weren't lazy. They just didn't spend any time figuring.

If I saw a stand of cottonwoods with limbs hanging out over a creek, I'd go look, figuring that a lot of people would pass it by, not wanting to get their feet wet looking for deadwood. Or I'd tie the Mustang loosely to a plum thicket and get scratched up crawling to find deadwood at its center.

"I am getting pretty good at finding firewood," I said quietly one morning.

Mrs. Kyler nodded. "Indeed you are. But you know what you'll be picking up for the cookfire before much longer, don't you?" She was stirring the eggs—the pork fat was beginning to snap and sizzle.

I wrinkled my nose. "Buffalo dung. That's what I heard Polly telling Julia. Is it true?"

She nodded. "You look for the dried-out ones. It won't be any worse than dry cow manure, I'm sure. It's just grass, after all."

I made another face, and she winked at me. "I have gloves you can borrow, and a bag. You won't have to touch it much."

I smiled at her, then turned back to the fire. I moved the skillet to place a Y-shaped piece of wood on the flames. The skillet didn't want to sit flat when I put it back. Mrs. Kyler handed me a smooth flat stone—part of her kitchen. I set one side of the skillet on it and let the new little log take the rest of the weight.

"You're a good hand to have on the journey," Mrs. Kyler said.

I blushed and mumbled a thanks.

"Are the girls being nicer to you yet?"

The question caught me off guard even though it shouldn't have. I had noticed her watching her granddaughters when I was close by. They almost never said a word to me, just ran off together, giggling and skipping if they weren't tired. When we had covered a lot of miles, they walked slower, their heads close together and whispering.

I looked at Mrs. Kyler. The short answer was no, they were less nice with every passing day. "They're fine," I fibbed. "We don't play much because I don't have time, always taking care of the Mustang. And you know they're busy with all their chores, too."

She shrugged. "I don't know what's wrong with them," she said.

I didn't answer. I was pretty sure I had puzzled out why the girls didn't like me—but I didn't want to tell Mrs. Kyler. It was partly because I was a stranger and they were protective of their friendships. They didn't want me wiggling my way in between any of them, trying to act like I belonged. But it was more than that. There were two other reasons.

I think I scared them in an odd way. I was an orphan. I was a walking example of their own worst worries—especially on this journey, no one knowing what was going to happen, who might not make it to the end.

I knew they were jealous of me, too, in a way. After all, I got to spend a lot more time with their grandmother than they did lately because they were as busy with chores as I was—in their own families' camps. They saw me laughing with Mrs. Kyler, joshing and teasing while we worked.

"I can insist they include you more," Mrs. Kyler said.

I came out of my thoughts and shook my head vehemently. "They'll really hate me if you do that," I blurted out before I could stop myself.

Mrs. Kyler tilted her head and stared at me a moment before she went back to tending the skillet. "I feel like I should give them a talking-to," she said quietly.

"Please don't," I begged. But then I pressed my lips together. I didn't want to make things worse by sounding so desperate about it.

"I have something for you," Mrs. Kyler said. She walked around to the front of the wagon and opened the carry box under the seat. When she came back, I saw she had a pink bonnet in her hands. "I stitched it up out of one of my old aprons. I hope you like pink."

I nodded. I did like pink well enough, but I hated bonnets. The way the coal-bucket face-shade stuck out, you couldn't see much to either side unless you turned your head way around. But I knew she meant well.

I took it and admired the stitching and thanked her twice. She was kind, and I was grateful to be traveling with her. I tucked the bonnet in my blanket roll so it would be safe. She saw me putting it away.

She frowned. "I can't make you wear it, but your skin will darken from the sun."

I nodded. "I know. I just hate the strings under my chin and the way you have to turn half way round to see what is going on. The Mustang wouldn't like it either, I am sure, and—"

She laughed and I didn't bother to finish my list of excuses. "I hate them, too," she told me. "But later on, when the sun gets fierce, you might want it."

"I'll keep it forever just because you made it," I said, without knowing I was going to say it. It sounded silly, the way it came out, but Mrs. Kyler smiled, and I knew she had understood it the way I'd meant it.

"The Mustang is holding his weight," I said after a minute, to change the subject. "I try real hard to find him extra grazing every day."

Mrs. Kyler nodded approvingly. She was a horse-woman, after all. "So are ours so far," she said. "Andrew manages to let them graze every few hours, then he'll trot them hard to catch up. The rest of the boys have been running the spare oxen closer to the wagon."

I smiled. When she said "the boys," she meant her grown sons. They had only granddaughters so far.

"Mary?"

Mrs. Kyler looked up. Andrew's wife was standing at the edge of the firelight. She had baby Rachel on her hip. "Yes, Hannah?" Mrs. Kyler answered.

I glanced up. It was almost light out. I could see Rachel's pouty little mouth and her big round eyes.

"What is it?" Mrs. Kyler asked, and her voice was full of concern.

It was only then that I looked at Hannah instead of her baby and saw that her face was tight and angry.

"Remember Snow? The white cat the girls brought along?"

Mrs. Kyler nodded. "Of course. She came from one of our barn cat's litters."

Hannah let out a long breath. "She's been running around a while every night. They just open the box and let her roam around a little."

Without speaking, Mrs. Kyler pulled the skillet off the fire and went to knock gently on the side of the wagon. Inside, Mr. Kyler woke and turned over, then got up. We could all hear the wooden wagon bed creaking as he stood up to stretch.

"I am hoping you aren't going to tell me that a coyote has gotten the cat," Mrs. Kyler said, turning back.

Hannah took a deep breath. "Well, they couldn't find it last night. They looked for an hour or more before Ellen could get Polly to go to bed. Once she was quiet, Julia and the little ones gave up, too."

Hannah glanced at me, and I lowered my eyes for a moment, then lifted them again and met her gaze. I didn't want her to think that I had had anything to do with the cat being killed.

"Oh dear," Mrs. Kyler said. "That sounds like a coyote."

Hannah shook her head. "No. That would be better. It would at least make sense."

Mrs. Kyler tilted her head. "What do you mean?"

Rachel started to fuss, and Hannah shifted her from one hip to the other. When she looked up again, her eyes were shiny with tears. "We found Snow this morning, dead. The girls are all crying and devastated. But the odd thing is that there wasn't a tooth mark on her. A rock killed her."

Mrs. Kyler was filling the tins now, and she looked up. "A rock?"

Hannah nodded. "Yes, ma'am. Someone threw a rock."

My stomach went tight.

"It's just so odd," she said. "We found the blood-ied stone right beside her. Someone killed the poor thing for no good reason at all. Why in the world would anyone do that?"

I eased in a long breath, and the boy's name came into my mind. Grover. His friend in Des Moines had called him Grover.

CHAPTER SIX

🐾 🐾 🐾

*The little one is scared of something. Her scent tells me
that, but I can see no new danger near. I am watchful.
If something tries to harm her, I will fight.*

I started leading the Mustang toward the back
of the wagon line to graze every morning once
Mrs. Kyler was packed and we were ready to go. That
meant I had to pass all the Kyler wagons, which
meant I had to nod and smile at Polly and Hope and
Julia and their parents, but I didn't care anymore. I
still didn't have it all quite straight, who was related
to whom—I didn't care about that, either.

What I wanted desperately to do was avoid seeing Grover. I wanted to think that he might have
just been fooling around trying to scare the cat,

that it had somehow been an accident, but I was pretty sure it hadn't been. I didn't want any trouble with him. All I wanted was to get to Oregon. It seemed safest to see him only from a distance and only when I had to.

The days slid past like the grassland we were traveling through. The Mustang and I walked from daybreak to late afternoon every single-bingle day, and my chores lasted start to finish and beyond. Everyone's did. As the oxen plodded on endlessly, it sometimes felt to me like we were standing still and the land was rolling beneath our feet, around and around, making the wagon wheels turn.

We made fair mileage almost every day, Mr. Teal said. Three wagons had stained one wheel spoke with India ink. Those families always had someone watching, someone counting how many times the spoke came past the top of the wheel. Then they would multiply the measurement of the wheel's rim by how many times it had turned around, and figure up how many miles from that.

I would never have been able to do it—I couldn't stare at anything for hours as a time without forgetting what I was doing. I was grateful that someone could, though. Every evening, the word of how far we had come spread through the camp, each person who heard it telling a few others. Our first day we had come only eleven miles. The second day we'd come nearly eighteen. We made twenty miles some days.

The best family for wheel watching was the Taylors. They had five children older than ten, and they all took turns so none of them got too cross-eyed from staring. Everyone appreciated it. It lightened everyone's hearts to know that the miles were passing, that a few more had been taken from the total of two thousand.

On the days when broken wheels or missing milk cows or any of the thousands of things that could go wrong *did* go wrong—the tiny mileage at the end of the day made us all resolve to work harder, to make better distance the next day.

Every evening after supper, I led the Mustang as far from camp as I had to in order to find fresh, un-grazed grass. I kept him out until dusk. Some places, grass was hard to find. It all depended on how many wagon parties had used that route before us and how big they had been. All the children around my age worked at herding the stock, competing for the best grass in places where there wasn't much.

I brought the Mustang back over the wagon tongue and into the circle of wagons every evening as soon as Andrew Kyler brought his horses in.

Once the mares were there, the Mustang was easy to settle for the night. He was always so glad to see them. He greeted them like it had been a month of Sundays since he had seen them last. He circled, snuffling in their breath, rubbing his muzzle on their shoulders, standing close. Midnight and Delia seemed happy to be near him, too.

I was so glad Hiram had sold the mares to Andrew so they had ended up coming on the journey. It was like having a little bit of Iowa and home with me, in a way. And as cruel as Mr. Stevens had been to me, he had been even worse to his animals. The mares were better off with Andrew Kyler any day.

Thanks to the mares and the Mustang's affection for them, I nearly always slept through until morning without worrying much about him now. The Mustang was so important to me. He was about as good a friend as I could ever remember having.

I spent nearly every waking hour walking with him. I talked to him more and more as the days passed. There were things that worried me, things that wore out my patience, and things that scared me. I was glad to be able to complain to someone who wouldn't think less of me for it.

I had been walking a little ways apart from the wagons from the beginning, and now I was hanging back to keep from having any contact with Grover. I had to make sure he had no reason and no opportunity to hurt the Mustang. The very thought of it made me so angry that my fists would ball up and my throat would ache.

We kept following the Platte River. It was strange, a mile or two wide in places and rarely much over six inches deep. Mrs. Kyler tried to wash a batch of shirts in it one morning and they ended up caked with sandy mud.

"Too thin to plow, too thick to drink," people were saying. I laughed the first few times I heard it. After that we had all learned how true it was, and it was no longer funny.

The Platte River wound around in great, sweeping arcs beneath a sky so blue that it looked painted. Mr. Teal kept us moving, following the river. When the grass looked better on the other side, we crossed, if there was enough hard sand on the bottom to make it possible. Then a few days later, we'd cross back.

We could see mountains on the westward horizon some days. They grew steadily bigger as the oxen plodded toward them. I remembered the name from listening to Mr. Barrett. The Rocky Mountains. The Rockies. That would be a hard part of the journey, I knew. Seeing them made me uneasy, but I pushed the thoughts from my mind.

One sunny morning a few days later, we saw Mormon families at a distance, traveling on the south bank of the Platte. We could tell them from all others two ways: some of the wagons were towing cannons, and we could see the man-pulled carts among the wagons.

When we passed anyone, Mr. Teal always raised a hand in greeting—many others did, too, but there were a few who glared in the direction of the Mormons and called them devil worshipers. It was such a terrible thing to say about anyone that it took my breath away.

Not everyone had gone to church on Sunday back home. The Stevenses never had. We'd had to sit and listen to Mr. Stevens read the Bible in a voice so dull and so boring that it was like hearing a list of farm chores recited. But my parents had been churchgoers, and many of the neighbors were, and no one ever really agreed about what the Bible meant on every subject.

Still, they had all gotten along more or less. No one had been afraid of anyone like people seemed to fear the Mormons. I couldn't see why. They all just looked like any old Iowa farm family to me.

"I'd like to talk to a Mormon one day," I said to the Mustang one morning. He lifted his head and then ducked his muzzle to avoid a buzzing deerfly. It looked like he had nodded. Then he shook his mane like he was disagreeing.

I laughed aloud. "I would, though. I bet they are the same as everyone else any way that matters much."

The Mustang lowered his head and rubbed his ears on my shoulder so hard it hurt. I looked at the fly welts on the thin skin at the base of his ears. Deerflies and no-see-ums were hatching. The mosquitoes were getting bad at night, too. The Platte was so shallow and flowed so slowly that bugs thrived along the banks.

"You walking at the back now?" Mr. Kyler said to me that evening. I nodded.

"Any particular reason why?"

I shrugged, hoping he wouldn't ask twice. I couldn't prove what I thought about Grover.

Mr. Kyler sipped at his coffee and looked up at the darkening sky. "Probably best not to get too far from the wagons."

"It's been hard to find good grass this whole past week," I said, defending myself. "I've had to take the Mustang farther and farther from the track to find anything much."

I waited for him to blow on his coffee, then sip it again. Then he looked at me. "Jack Taylor says he saw some Indians this morning."

I caught my breath. "He did?"

"Not long after we started out. They were mounted, a line of fifteen or twenty of them at a great distance. They just watched us go past. They value a good horse, people say."

I blinked. "You think they'd steal the Mustang?"

He shrugged. "Or just pester you to trade him away. Best not to be caught out on your own. Jack had no idea which tribe it was. Just stay closer, Katie."

I swallowed hard. *Indians.* I knew perfectly well that most people going west met Indians. There were stories about the Indian men helping at river crossings, giving widows food, being neighborly in most every way. Still, the idea scared me. They were just so...unknown.

"Most folks trade with them for food or stock," Mr. Kyler was saying. "We brought beads and mirrors. Mr. Teal told us he brought a few steel knives for that purpose. I suspect they'd want good knives more than anything." He sighed. "The guidebook said to bring beads and mirrors." He reached out and patted my head, and it made me think of Hiram. "You stay close, hear me?"

"I'll be careful," I said aloud. "I will."

Mr. Kyler nodded. "See that you do. No one has time to mind any of you children like should be done."

He leaned over his coffee cup again. I couldn't tell if he was finished talking. He reminded me a little of my father that way. Pa hadn't talked a great deal, but when he had, people would stop and listen; then he'd go quiet again.

I thought about my father, and, for an instant, I

couldn't quite picture him. Almost, but not exactly. I turned away from the fire as though I was turning to warm my backside, but I was really hiding tears. My mind went spinning in circles like creek current. Why couldn't I see my father clearly in my mind? What had his ears looked like, his nose, his hands?

I let out a long, slow breath. I could picture his hands perfectly, the big fingers working tiny threads to tie his fishing flies or holding a Sidley's bottle to nursemaid an orphaned calf. But his face wouldn't come.

I started to picture my mother and sister, then excused myself and walked away from the fire into the darkness instead. What if I couldn't conjure up their images, either. What if they were all fading in my memories? I shivered, more scared by that thought than any talk about Indians could have made me. The night seemed too big, too dark.

I glanced back. Mr. Kyler was leaning forward at the waist to stare at the fire. He hadn't even noticed my leaving, I was pretty sure.

"I guess he has other things on his mind," I told the Mustang when I found him. "Like Pa usually did."

The Mustang sidled closer to me, nudging me gently with his muzzle. I hugged him hard, crying silently, knowing that no one would see. It was dark; there was no moon at all.

I knew there were lots of everyday things to be worrying about, but all I could do right then was miss my family worse than I ever had before.

CHAPTER SEVEN

🎭 🎭 🎭

The little one stood with the mares and me last
night for a long time. She is welcome.

*I*t was getting hot as spring faded into summer. The sun baked the treeless earth in a
circle that extended to the horizon in every direction.

The week after Mr. Kyler had talked to me, I
stayed within shouting distance of the wagons.
Then one day we forded the Platte at about noon
because the grass on the north side was tall and
green. The oxen had had scant feed for a week, so
Mr. Teal gave a long enough dinner break for
people to unhitch and let their teams eat for a

couple of hours. I led the Mustang a good distance away to stay clear of the oxen.

Just as the Mustang was getting settled, Mr. Kyler whistled between his teeth, a high shrill sound that made everyone look up at once. He pointed.

I saw something so strange it took me a few minutes to realize what I was seeing. I heard Mrs. Craggett make a startled sound and knew she had just figured it out as well.

What had looked at first like dark, plowed farm fields—where there should have been nothing but prairie grass—had inexplicably come alive with movement. They weren't farm fields at all.

It was a herd of bison—the buffalo we had all heard about. I led the Mustang at an angled trot, back toward the wagons. Everyone came in close, even though the huge animals were a good distance off.

We stared as they got nearer. They were huge, but that wasn't what scared me. I had seen farm bulls almost as big—Hiram's beautiful Ayrshire oxen had been as heavy, almost.

The amazing thing was how *many* buffalo there were. Imagine seeing a flock of sparrows big enough to turn the sky dark. It was like that. The buffalo darkened the ground, hiding the green of the grass with the deep brown of their bodies. I could smell them—a smell like cattle, but wilder, mixed the constant sweet odor of the endless grass.

The Mustang wasn't scared of the buffalo. But he kept an eye on them, and his ears ticked back and forth, listening to the low rumbling of their hooves on the earth.

For nearly two hours, we stood watching the buffalo herd pass us. A dust cloud arced above the heavy animals, coloring the sky a dusty rouge. When they were finally gone, like a brown storm, ebbing in the north, we started up again.

For a long time, no one said anything. Then everyone began to talk at once. When we crossed the ground the herd had walked, I stared. Their hooves had flattened the grass and pitted the topsoil.

⚜ ⚜ ⚜

The next day, we took another long dinner break for the same reason: deep grass. I tied the Mustang to the wagon, loosely, so he could graze while I helped Mrs. Kyler cook and serve the meal. Then we repacked the jockey box, and I started to leave.

"Katie, give me ten more minutes," Mrs. Kyler said. "Help me spread the quilts out." I nodded and walked with her to the back of the wagon. All the women would be taking this extra time to clean a little, I was sure. We rarely got a chance to do anything but the necessities.

Mrs. Kyler had nice quilts. She had made many of them, but some were old, from her mother and grandmother. We unfolded them and laid them out at the rear of the wagon, letting the tall grass support the cloth, fresh air passing beneath it.

"Mary? Katie?" Mr. Kyler said from behind us. We both turned. Instead of speaking, he pointed. I followed his gesture, wondering if he had spotted more buffalo. He hadn't. There was a line of Indians on the other side of the river. One of them lifted his hand in greeting.

I saw Mr. Teal mount, then spur his horse into a gallop, heading down the line of wagons. "Everyone stay calm and friendly. Pass the word," he shouted. "They've got a buffalo haunch, it looks like. Maybe we can trade for a little fresh meat!"

I heard people calling out what he had said, like some kind of weird echo moving through the line.

The word *buffalo* was repeated with as much amazement as any of the rest. I am not sure it had occurred to even one of the men to try to kill a buffalo when we had seen them. If it had, no one had risked stampeding the massive herd by shooting.

I stood as still as a stone, staring at the Indians, until Mr. Kyler nudged me.

"Katie, get that horse of yours around to the far side of the wagon. No sense showing him off." He walked to the driver's bench and reached beneath it for his rifle. He leaned it up against the wheel, then stepped away from it.

I ran to untie the Mustang's rope, then glanced over my shoulder. Mr. Teal had reined in and was gesturing at the Indian men from our side of the river.

"Should we close up the wagon or—" Mrs. Kyler began.

"I think it'll be just fine, Mary," Mr. Kyler said evenly. "We have anything we could trade for meat?"

Mrs. Kyler didn't answer, but I heard the wagon creak, and I knew she had climbed inside to rummage through her things. She came out with a pair of sewing scissors and some mirrors.

I led the Mustang over the wagon tongue, trying not to make him trot. I didn't want to call attention to him.

"Here they come," I heard Mr. Kyler say.

I positioned the Mustang close to the wagon, then inched forward, trying to see. He followed me, of course. I faced him, and he stopped. Turning back, I leaned out, just far enough to see that the Indian men were coming across the Platte now, galloping their horses. The man in front made a long, wavering cry as he came. His leather shirt had feathers tied into the fringe, and it looked fine and handsome as he rode.

I stared. I had never seen anyone ride like that in my whole life. It was as though the man and the horse had somehow joined in the middle and were one creature now. The man who had made the first gesture of greeting was the first one across. The last one was the man leading the packhorse that carried the meat.

The first man reined in, his big bay horse sliding to a halt in front of Mr. Teal. The others stopped a little ways off and waited, watching us with as much interest as we were watching them.

Mr. Teal sat his horse easily, smiling. After a moment, I could hear their voices, but the words were completely foreign to me. Mr. Teal didn't say much; he seemed to know only a little of the Indian man's language, but the few words he managed must have been the right ones.

The Indian man turned and said something to his friends. The man leading the packhorse came forward. Mr. Teal reached into his saddlebag and took out something I couldn't see clearly, just a flash of shiny metal as he leaned forward in his saddle to hand it to the Indian man.

"Looks like we won't need your scissors or the mirrors, Mary," I heard Mr. Kyler say. "Put 'em where you can get them easier next time, though."

"I will," Mrs. Kyler said. "Aren't they wonderful?" she added.

I heard Mr. Kyler make a little sound of agreement. "You can't help but admire their riding. I wish I could talk with them."

The Mustang nudged me from behind, and I stumbled forward, then scrambled back. I circled him, bringing him close against the wagon. Then I inched forward again, trying to see.

Two Indian men had dismounted and were carrying the meat to set it down in tall grass. They straightened and walked to rinse their hands in the river before they remounted.

They had more skin showing than I had ever seen in my life, but they walked as though they were wearing the finest suits and collars in the country. They were all fairly tall, it looked like, and most of them were handsome of feature, too.

In less than a minute, the two men who had carried the meat were back astride their horses, swinging up with more grace than I'd ever seen any person mount a horse.

They were gathering their reins, turning to talk to each other as they sat their horses, and I was sure they were about to go back across the river— but they didn't. Instead, the man who had traded with Mr. Teal started forward, toward us, and the men behind him followed his lead.

I heard a little gasp go through the women in the party, and saw more than one man back up, getting closer to the rifles that most of them had brought out. The Indian men had been nothing but polite, but they looked so different from what any of us were used to, it was hard not to be afraid of them.

The men walked their horses forward, staring at us just as we stared at them. They angled toward the gap between the Kylers' wagon and the McMahons', just in front of us.

I ducked back and led the Mustang along the back side of the wagon, intending to circle around and then watch the Indian men ride off. I had to swing wider than I wanted to because of Mrs. Kyler's quilts, and I found myself suddenly blundering right into the path of the first Indian man. He reined in his horse and scowled at me. Then his expression changed as he looked past me and saw the Mustang.

The Indian man's horse squealed and reared, and he pulled it around, getting control over it again. It made another high-pitched squealing sound and shook its head, prancing sideways.

The Mustang answered, his head coming up, his ears flat against his head.

"Katie, get out of the way!" Mr. Kyler shouted. "It's a stallion."

The Indian shouted something, dragging at his

rawhide rein as his horse struggled against it.

The Mustang pulled the rope out of my hands as he reared. I staggered back, almost falling.

The Indian man reached forward and grabbed his mount's ear, pulling it hard, but the stallion didn't even seem to notice.

"Katie, get out of the way; get back!" Mr. Kyler shouted. Mrs. Kyler screamed as the Indian's horse plunged forward, his ears flattened and his teeth bared.

The Mustang leapt to one side and galloped a few strides, then whirled back and faced the Indian's horse, his neck arched. The Indian man pulled his mount in another tight circle, but I knew it wasn't going to work. Unless we could get them farther apart, they were going to fight.

"No!" I shouted, running toward the Mustang, waving my hands to make him see me, to make him listen to me.

He reared and I slowed, then went forward again the instant his hooves were on the ground. He snorted and pawed at the earth, still looking past me.

I was shaking, terrified, but I started talking, louder than usual, trying to reason with the Mustang.

"There's no reason to fight," I pleaded. "He isn't going to stay here, and he isn't going to get your mares. He's leaving. They just want to go."

I heard the Indian's stallion squeal again and the heavy thudding of his hooves on the ground, but I didn't turn around. The Mustang was looking at me now, at *me*.

"You don't have to do anything but hold still," I told him, hearing how foolish it sounded, but glad that he was listening to me now, his head a little lower. I reached out and took the lead rope in my hands, and the Mustang lowered his head to touch my cheek with his muzzle. I glanced back. The Indian man had managed to get his horse to turn aside. The horse's ears were still back, but he had stopped squealing.

I pulled the Mustang around, leading him away as fast as I could, circling him when he balked. He reared again, raking at the air with his front hooves, and I jumped back, then stepped forward again when his hooves struck the earth.

I rubbed his neck with the flat of my palm, talking a blue streak, explaining over and over that the Indian's bay was leaving, that he was no threat to any of us. Finally, he walked a straight line and lowered his head a little. His nostrils were still flared, but the wildness was leaving his eyes.

When I looked back, I saw a ring of faces. Half the wagon party had gathered to watch. The Indian man sat his horse easily and gracefully; he pivoted the horse so tightly that he had to half rear to spin around. At that instant his eyes met mine, and he smiled, gesturing at the Mustang.

I was unsure what his gesture meant, and I had no idea what was rude and what was polite, but I didn't want to offend him. It had been my fault, not his. I had been so eager to see, not to miss anything. I wanted to apologize, but I could only lift my hand and smile back at him.

He held my eyes an instant longer, then he was turning again, shouting to his friends, leading the way as they rode out of our camp. The big bay sprang into a long-striding gallop that none of the other horses could match. The Indian man didn't look back.

My heart was going like a rabbit's in the dog yard. I blushed at all the people staring at me. A few of the boys whistled through their teeth and clapped like I had meant to put on a show of some kind. The Mustang danced a little at the noise. Mr. Kyler shushed them.

My knees shaking, I led the Mustang away from the wagons so he could settle down and graze again—and so I could watch the Indians ride away. I glanced back once to see the crowd breaking up, everyone going back to their work, only a few still watching me. After a few minutes, I thought to look for Grover among the ones still standing and talking about the Indians' visit with Mr. Kyler. If he had been, he'd lost interest; he wasn't there.

That night it clouded over and started to rain. Lying under the wagon, I was glad the Mustang had the mares to stand close to for warmth. I was grateful that the Kylers were so good to me. And I wondered if the Indian men had made it home before the storm started.

CHAPTER EIGHT

✿ ✿ ✿

*The two-leggeds brought another stallion close.
I was ready to fight. The little one stopped me. She is
wise. It is always better not to fight.*

*T*he sun blazed overhead. Every day brought more walking, more seed burrs in my dress hem, more miles of the shallow, warm-water Platte, more of the endless ocean of waving grass. We stayed on the south side, where the grazing was better. Most of the stock was holding weight. The Kylers lost one ox that just dropped in its traces. It took an hour to get the harness off and back the wagon away from the carcass so another ox could be harnessed in its place.

The day after that, it began to rain. It stormed

for ten days off and on. Even when it let up and we could travel, we could still see thicker clouds to the northwest. The storms were noisy and windy, but it didn't cool down much. The air got steamy and thick, and we saw sheets of purple-black rain hanging over the western horizon. For the first time since we had begun traveling beside it, the Platte began to rise.

"The river forks a few miles up, north and south," Mr. Teal said one night. "We have to end up north of it to go on up into the Wyoming country and Fort Laramie. If we wait, we'll have both forks to cross."

A murmuring went through the men.

"You saying we should cross it now," Mr. Kyler asked, "not wait for the water to go down?"

Mr. Teal nodded. "It ain't that deep, and the bottom won't have had time to wash out that much. If we wait, it could get worse for a week or more, not better."

I listened to the men talking to one another in low voices. The river *was* high. I could hear it rushing past in the darkness beyond the wagon circle. Mr. Teal was the last one to say anything that was loud enough for me to hear. "Rise early and pack tight," he shouted over the murmuring. "We cross tomorrow.

It rained again that night, a wild storm with lightning that cracked the sky, scaring the stock into milling around inside the wagon circle. I checked the Mustang four or five times—he wasn't as spooked as the mares were. They were both pressed close to him, shivery in the wind and rain.

The next morning, Andrew took his stock out of the wagon circle early. I hurried to finish helping Mrs. Kyler, then ran to tie the lead to the Mustang's halter. I led him off toward the back of the wagon train, as had become my habit. I headed toward the river, wanting to get a look at it. I came around the last wagon and saw a lot of the menfolk lined up, talking, staring out at the brown water.

I walked the Mustang past them, going slow, trying to overhear.

"Why in tarnation didn't we cross a week ago while it was low?" Andrew Kyler was asking. Mr. McMahon was nodding, but I couldn't hear what he said.

I walked the Mustang a little ways off and let

him set himself to grazing. I was tired—I had been awake half the night or more, so I sat in the grass holding the long lead rope in one hand, looking off to the west.

This whole thing made me nervous. Every time we had crossed the Platte before, I had simply led the Mustang along beside the wagons. It wasn't any more scary than crossing a creek back home; it was just much wider. Mr. Teal had said there could be quicksand mud, so soft a person could get stuck in it—but no one had found any. I'd just stayed in the path of the ones in front.

There were more clouds gathering to the west this morning—dark clouds. I looked out over the water. There was foam on it now, and the color had darkened to a muddy brown, nearly as brown as the Missouri had been.

I fiddled with the tattered hem of my dress, my eyes heavy from lack of sleep. The Mustang always grazed quietly now, and I knew it wasn't likely that he would shy at anything. The sky overhead was clouded thinly; it wasn't going to rain for a while anyway. I leaned back on my elbows and I might have dozed off if the shouting hadn't started.

I snapped up straight, listening. The Mustang lifted his head, too. There were several voices. I got to my feet and looked back down the bank. Mr. Teal was standing at the center of a ring of men. Mr. McMahon was talking loudly, jabbing his finger in the air as he spoke. His wife stood off to one side, and I could see her lips moving, finishing his sentences the way she always did. Her face was flushed, she was as angry as her husband was.

Mr. Teal shook his head and started to walk off, but Mr. McMahon called him back, and they went on talking, their voices lowered again.

Mrs. McMahon started away, still glaring over her shoulder at Mr. Teal. The men's voices had calmed, and I couldn't hear them anymore. I wanted to lead the Mustang closer, to eavesdrop; but I knew I'd get scolded for it, so I didn't. Instead, I led the Mustang along, drifting toward camp.

All the men I passed were grumbling. It was clear how upset they were. It was also clear that they were packing up and getting ready to cross the river.

"It probably isn't that deep," Mr. Kyler was telling his wife as I led the Mustang back into their camp.

She was frowning, staring at the sky to the west.

"If this storm upstream was as bad as it was here—"

"And it ain't over, not by a long shot," Mr. Kyler interrupted her, squinting to see better. "If we wait, it could keep us on this side long enough to starve the stock."

It looked to me like the storm was just getting started. The clouds were the color of charcoal, almost. I almost said it aloud, then I bit my lip. It was not my place to argue with either one of them.

"Got your things all wrapped up, Katie?" Mrs. Kyler asked me.

I shook my head and tied the Mustang loosely to the side of the wagon so he could nibble at the grass, then I ran to shake the grass and dirt out of my bedding. I folded it, damp though it was, and carried it into the wagon. All our bedding and most of our clothes were damp. They would stay that way until the sun came out for a few days.

I checked my little bundle, feeling my mother's book and the one I had bought in Council Bluff through the thin blanket. I had barely read since we'd left Council Bluff. I wondered if the Kyler girls were reading the magazines that Annie had gotten for them.

I was so chilly and so worried that I found myself daydreaming. Maybe once I was settled in my uncle Jack's house, I could read to his children every night. The idea made me smile as I climbed out over the wagon gate.

I looked at the river. The Platte wasn't half as big as the Missouri. And it couldn't be that deep. The banks were so wide it had just spread out.

"I'm ready," I called out, jumping off the wooden step at the back of the wagon.

Mrs. Kyler nodded and smiled at me. I looked around. Mr. Kyler had gone.

"Benton said they're trying to decide where to cross," she told me, pointing. "But they're still arguing, I think."

I turned to see the men walking along the edge of the water, talking and gesturing. Mr. Teal was there and Mr. McMahon, and Mr. Silas and a dozen others, but they kept their voices low, and we couldn't hear anything they were saying.

Mr. Kyler finally came back. "We're going to go on across," he said evenly. "Down there a little ways." He gestured.

I heard Mrs. Kyler sigh. Mr. Kyler heard her,

too, and he put his arm around her shoulders. "Don't worry, Mary. Mr. Teal waded out nearly halfway. It isn't that deep. We aren't even going to string up the ropes."

I breathed out in relief, but then he turned to me. "But it's too deep for you. No one is going to walk stock across, Katie. Andrew and the boys are going to run the horses across last."

I started to argue, but he shushed me.

"Katie, I want you to ride in the wagon and leave that stallion to the men."

I lifted my chin, stunned into silence. Then I found my voice. "What if he runs off?"

He shook his head. "Child, Andrew knows how to handle a horse. The mares won't run, and the stallion won't leave them behind. I want you in the wagon." The last sentence was a command.

"He's right, Katie," Mrs. Kyler said before I could speak. "We promised Hiram to get you safe to Oregon and we don't take promises lightly in the Kyler family."

"But I'll be fine walking him!" I managed.

They both shook their heads.

"I'm going to take him over to Andrew right

now," Mr. Kyler insisted, then turned to go.

I started to run toward the Mustang, but Mrs. Kyler caught me in her arms and held me tight. Mr. Kyler walked up to the Mustang slowly and untied the lead rope. He tugged it lightly, and the Mustang followed him. "See?" he said, glancing back. "He's gentler than you think he is."

"Andrew will take good care of him, Katie," Mrs. Kyler said. "You know he will."

I felt my heart miss a beat, then start again. I wriggled against her, and she let me slide to the ground. I was breathing hard, my heart slamming against my ribs. I felt almost ill. It was wrong for me to be separated from the Mustang. He *needed* me. What would happen if he did get spooked?

Mrs. Kyler set her hand lightly on my shoulder, and I moved away from her. I watched Mr. Kyler leading the Mustang away for as long as I could stand it, then I ran to the back of the wagon and climbed in. I slumped down against my blanket and started to sob. I used my old trick, the one I learned at the Stevenses' house. I opened my mouth wide, letting the convulsions of breath pass out of my body almost silently. If Mrs. Kyler heard me, she left me alone, and for that I was grateful.

After a time, I managed to stop crying, and I stood up to straighten my dress as much as I could. Then I went down the ladder and forced myself to look toward the milling band of stock that Andrew Kyler and his brothers were herding. They were just holding them until the wagons were ready to move. I had seen them do it dozens of times. And there was the Mustang, grazing quietly beside Delia and Midnight.

"You ready?" It was Mr. Kyler, behind me. I whirled around.

"Yes," I told him. My voice was high and patchy. He was kind enough to act like he hadn't noticed. I looked back at the Mustang. He seemed perfectly content. He wasn't looking around for me.

"That horse loves you as much as a horse knows how to love a human," Mr. Kyler said. "Now, let's get across the river.

I dragged in a long breath. Mr. Teal was riding the outside of the wagon circle, talking to the men as he went. We were supposed to line up just like usual, except that the front wagons would turn sharp right to cross dead-on—not at a slant.

"May I sit on the bench?" I asked Mr. Kyler. I wanted to be able to see the river, to see that the Mustang was all right with the mares still.

He nodded.

"Polly or Julia want to come with us?" Mrs. Kyler asked. "Or Hope?"

Mr. Kyler shook his head. "I didn't ask, but they're all settled in their own wagons, Mary. Let's leave it alone."

She glanced at me and nodded, then smiled cheerfully. "Hop up, then, they're about ready."

Sitting on the wagon bench was strange at first. The wagon swayed and rolled with the lay of the land. We were about halfway back in the line, so by the time the Kylers' oxen waded into the water, we'd watched so many wagons make it safely across, I wasn't a bit scared. I just wanted the whole wagon line to get across fast so that I could lead the Mustang again.

As the oxen waded out and struggled for footing in the mud, the sky to the west rumbled quietly. The sparks of lightning made me look up. The dark clouds in the west were coming our way now.

Mr. Kyler popped his whip, but the crack was lost in the next round of crackling thunder. It wasn't loud or close, and no rain was falling, but it made me uneasy. I twisted around on the seat, trying to get a glimpse of the Mustang.

The wagon lurched and slid sideways for an instant. Mrs. Kyler gripped my arm, steadying me, then the wheels caught hold, and the oxen strained, moving the wagon up out of the water at last. Mr. Kyler reined in a few hundred feet from the river, falling into place behind Mr. McMahon's rig.

Mr. Teal was riding up and down the line, shouting advice and instruction to the drivers. I slid down off the seat and turned to watch the last of the wagons come across. Then I held my breath as Andrew and his brothers drove the stock forward.

Mr. Teal rode to the edge of the river. The Mustang was at the rear of the herd, nipping at the flanks of the mares to get them into the water. For a moment, it looked like he was doing the herding, not the Kylers.

"Turn them back!" Mr. Teal shouted. "Turn them back!"

He waved as he shouted, a big, sweeping arc of his arm, trying to get the herders' attention. From a distance it was easy to see that they weren't looking at him. They were watching the horses and mules, riding toward them slowly, forcing them into the water. I saw the Mustang plunge to a stop, looking upriver. Then he lunged forward again.

"Spread them out!" I heard Andrew shouting. "Don't push so hard! They'll step on one another."

Mr. Teal was spurring his horse into the water, roaring, waving one arm over his head, pointing upstream. I followed his gesture and understood at last. There was a wall of brown water coming, taller than a man, roiling with foam. I stared at it, unable to look away. The shouting and screaming around me blended into the sound of the river.

As the wall of water came closer, I saw tree limbs churning within it; then I caught a split-second glimpse of a wide, rough-barked trunk. The flash flood had uprooted a cottonwood tree.

I glanced at the far bank. Most of the horses were in the water now. The Mustang and the two mares were toward the rear of the herd, but they were standing belly-deep in the river. The Mustang was rearing, plunging in the water, driving the mares backward.

A sudden crack of thunder overhead was followed

by a blue-white flash of light. Mr. Teal's horse reared, its mouth open as it fought against the tight reins. It lost its footing on the mud and gravel on the river bottom and went down. An instant later it was struggling to get back up, thrashing at the water with its forehooves. Mr. Teal slid sideways in the saddle, and I saw him wrenching around to look upstream. Then the flash flood engulfed him and his horse.

Twenty men sprinted toward the river, shouting. The wave roared past, the tree inside it windmilling, its broken branches thrusting up out of the water, then disappearing again. It was swept onward, churning the water into foam, flinging up stones and gobbets of mud.

The Mustang had gotten the mares back to safety. There were three horses still in the river. One was dead. The other two were fighting to get out of the current.

I stared. Behind the wave, the water was deeper than it had been. Mr. Teal's horse was struggling to stand, whinnying in terror. It took the men on the bank a few seconds to plunge into the water, all of them glancing upstream every few seconds.

They dragged Mr. Teal back to the bank. There was blood trickling down one side of his face and soaking through the right leg of his trousers. His horse, by some miracle, seemed to be all right.

I looked across the river and saw the horses milling in the shallows, squealing and scared. Andrew and his brothers were all safe, reining their horses back and forth in the shallows, trying to keep the herd from scattering.

The Mustang was way off to one side, his eyes wide, his tail lashing back and forth. The mares stood near him, their heads up and their nostrils flared wide. The water level was dropping fast. I started running.

CHAPTER NINE

๛ ๛ ๛

The two-leggeds are sometimes stupid. Perhaps
they don't know about rivers for some reason.
I kept the mares safe until the little one found us.

*T*he Mustang had herded Delia and Midnight
far up on the bank by the time I got to the edge
of the water. The rest of the horses were frantic,
some of them plunging into deeper water, scattering as the men struggled to bunch them up and get
them out of the river.

I glanced back. The men were moving Mr. Teal
farther up the bank. Mrs. Kyler had a blanket and
was spreading it on the ground. People were shouting at one another, running back and forth.

Across the river Andrew was still riding circles

around the stock with his brothers, trying to force them back into a herd—all but the Mustang.

He had run the mares back even before Andrew had noticed the danger. He was standing apart from the others on the far bank with the mares, his head high, his eyes wide open and rimmed in white.

I knew the Kylers would forbid me to go back across, but I had to. I couldn't leave the Mustang with just the two mares off to one side like that. He was excited, and I could see the wild look in his eyes. If something spooked him, he could take off and I would never see him again.

I slid down the bank and waded in, watching the upstream side with every step. The water hadn't looked so deep on the wagon wheels, but it had risen, and it came almost to my chest in the deepest part. The current skidded me downstream and I was scared, but I managed to stay on my feet.

"Katieeee!" It was Mrs. Kyler—she had finally noticed what I was doing.

I didn't glance back. I was almost across, and I kept looking upstream, terrified that another drowned tree would come rolling toward me, but none did. I waded up out of the shallows, my dress plastered to my legs, water streaming out of my hair, shivering and weak-kneed.

"Stand easy," I called to the Mustang. "Just stand easy now."

I could hear the elder Kylers shouting at me and their sons yelling at the milling stock, but the rushing of the river dulled all the voices.

"I just need to come stand with you," I told the Mustang. I kept walking toward him. He was holding his head high, and his ears were twitching, but he never tried to back away from me. He stood still as I reached up to slip my hand through the halter. I longed for the lead rope, but it was coiled up inside the Kylers' wagon.

Andrew's horses were still skittish and circling at a gallop, scaring one another now that the real danger had passed. The Mustang lowered his head and the grassy smell of his breath—and its warmth—made me smile. "Will you come with me?" I asked him. "Maybe we should just get you across in case Andrew's horses decide to bolt."

He shook his mane and stamped a forehoof, splattering my legs with mud.

"I hope that means yes," I said as calmly as I could.

I looked up the river as far as I could see. There was nothing but the rushing brown water, the level dropping fast. Thunder rolled in the distance as I put a gentle, steady pressure on the halter, urging the Mustang forward.

He took a single step, then balked for a second; then he followed me again. The mares came along as though they were being led as well, one on either side of the Mustang, their heads even with his withers.

I could see a crowd on the far bank and was sure they had gathered around Mr. Teal. I hoped that he wasn't hurt as bad as it had looked.

The center of the river wasn't as scary with the Mustang next to me, with his weight and strength to anchor me in the rushing water. Midnight and Delia stuck close. Coming up the bank toward the wagons, I looked toward the circle of men again.

Then I saw Mrs. Kyler coming toward me. Her face was flushed and angry. "Katie, I know you love that horse, but you can't—"

"I'm fine though," I interrupted her as politely as I could. The Mustang tossed his head, and I was pulled off my feet for an instant. I ignored Mrs. Kyler's little gasp and gestured toward Mr. Teal.

"Is he hurt bad?"

"Benton says it looks like it," Mrs. Kyler told me. "One leg is all smashed up." I saw her eyes darken with worry, but she didn't say anything more. She just took Delia's halter strap and led her up the muddy bank. Midnight stayed close without being led at all. I followed with the Mustang.

We didn't go another foot westward that day. The menfolk circled the wagons a ways uphill from the river in case the storm caused more flash floods in the night. It was an unhappy camp, everyone worried about Mr. Teal, scared of the idea of being without a guide.

Mrs. Kyler knew a little about doctoring, and she straightened Mr. Teal's broken leg and splinted it to a plank. We all heard him screaming. It was awful.

It rained again that night, big pelting drops that made it impossible to keep a campfire lit and drove everyone into the wagons early. I brought the Mustang and the mares close to the wagon so they could shelter their faces some, then went to sit inside with the Kylers. None of the girls were there; it wasn't a night to go visiting.

The oil lamp burnt low while Mr. Kyler read

an almanac and Mrs. Kyler mended clothes. I read my mother's book, the words as familiar as the taste of beans and bacon.

The Kylers settled me into the feather bed. I sank into the softness and felt the whole long day's weariness settle on my bones. I closed my eyes and lay there, thinking. What would I have done if the Mustang had gotten away? And what would we do if Mr. Teal couldn't go on?

I thought about my uncle Jack and his family. I pretended I was already at their house, telling them about the whole long journey. They were listening to me, their eyes wide, his daughters sitting with their hands over their mouths, amazed at all my adventures....

"What?" I heard Mr. Kyler ask, his voice strained.

My imagined storytelling stopped instantly, and I was wide awake again, listening.

"I think they'll end up taking him back," Mrs. Kyler answered. It isn't just broken—the bone came through the skin. His knee was twisted so hard, it'll be swollen three times its size tomorrow. He is dizzy-headed. He can't ride or walk."

There was a long silence, and then Mr. Kyler

said, "We aren't anywhere near the rough part yet."

"I know," Mrs. Kyler said softly. Then, after a long pause, she sighed loud enough for me to hear. "Who do you think will carry him back?"

Mr. Kyler hesitated, and I could imagine him with his chin in his hand, thinking. "There's more than you think would like to go back given any excuse, and a few of the young men are talking about heading south to Mexico if the war lasts. Or Texas."

Mrs. Kyler made a soft, sad sound. "I hear them bottoming out, their spirits tired—and they know the worst is ahead yet. Some are afraid of the war spreading northward, too. What do you think on that?" Mrs. Kyler asked him.

He made a sound of disdain. "It's going to be a mess for years, I suspect, but it's a long ways off. Unless one of our boys decides to gallop off and volunteer, we won't be touched by it at all."

Mrs. Kyler hushed him. "Don't put anything in their heads, Benton. At least they are all married now; that always settles a man down."

My Kyler chuckled. "Worked that way for me," he said. I heard him kiss her on the cheek. They blew out the oil lamp and crawled into their bedding.

The rain let up, then came down hard again. The storm rocked the wagon, but the featherbed felt like I was sleeping on clouds after months of sleeping on the ground, and I knew the Mustang wouldn't set off in this weather—he was much too smart. I closed my eyes and fell into an exhausted sleep.

CHAPTER TEN

❦ ❦ ❦

The two-legged herd is separating.
I cannot understand why they would do this.

$\mathcal{T}$he next day, a group of seven wagons started back toward Council Bluff. Mr. Teal was in the back of one of them, padded by as many blankets and bedclothes as the party could spare.

Mrs. Kyler and I stood watching the wagons head back along the north side of the river. "They'll wait for the water to go down to cross back," she said. Then she was still a moment. "I only hope he makes it," she said quietly.

I looked at her. "You mean he might die?"

She nodded sadly. "He's hurt bad, Katie, bruises

and cracked ribs and the leg bone pierced his flesh from the inside out. The wound wasn't big, but it could sicken and go putrid. He needs rest, not a pounding in a wagon bed."

"Then why doesn't he just stay here for a while and..." I trailed off because I knew the answer to the question. No one wanted to stay here with him. Those who wanted to go on were afraid to take extra time. Those who had decided to go back wanted to go find land in Nebraska Territory before the summer was gone—or get settled in Council Bluff to wait the winter out, then try again for Oregon.

The wagons weren't even out of sight before I heard the first argument erupt. It was Mr. Silas. Now that Mr. Teal was gone, he saw no reason why he and his friends shouldn't be the first wagon in line, to make up for all the dust and mud they had eaten being last all this time.

No one argued too long with them. Most just wanted to get going. The men had their maps and guidebooks out all day—at the dinner stop, Mr. Kyler pulled out a compass I had never seen him use before.

At supper, after we had traveled along the Platte,

we came upon a mound of goods—a heavy bedstead and chairs, just piled beside the rutted road. Several of the women looked at the bedstead with longing, but no one so much as discussed picking it up. It was becoming all too clear how extra weight grated at the oxen's strength.

We had gone only seven or eight miles when another argument began. I was leading the Mustang out to graze and I slowed him to listen. Mr. Silas wanted to take shorter dinner stops. The McMahons—and every other family with little children—said they couldn't manage with less time.

"We need to elect a leader," Mr. Kyler said when the men had talked themselves to a resentful stand-still.

Mr. Silas made a sound of disgust. "And I suppose you think it ought to be you?"

Mr. Kyler looked surprised. "No, no. Someone younger, someone who knows about the trail ahead if we have anyone who does." He looked around the circle of faces.

Mr. McMahon cleared his throat. "I made a study of the guidebooks and the maps."

No one else spoke up.

By the time we broke camp, eight more wagons had decided to go back eastward, to travel hard and catch up with the party carrying Mr. Teal—or so they said. I wondered if any would try to join a wagon party with a guide if they met one.

One man and his pregnant wife decided to go back. So did a family whose youngest boy had fallen beneath a wagon wheel that crushed his ankle. But most of the others were clearly afraid the arguing would explode into fighting.

Grover's family decided to go on. For the first time, I heard their last name. It was Heldon. Mr. Heldon had a gaunt face and angry eyes. Mrs. Heldon looked exhausted. If Grover remembered me, he showed no sign of it. I started to hope he hadn't recognized me at all down by the Elkhorn River that day. Maybe he threw rocks at a dozen horses a day and had forgotten the incident completely?

The McMahons and the Kylers decided to keep going—and, of course, Mr. Silas and his men. There were two other wagons still going. The Craggetts— the woman with the milk cow and her husband— were in one, and the Taylors, the mileage keeper and his family, in the other. They had three older boys and two girls a little older than I was. One of them was a pale child who rode in the wagon most of the time.

I listened to the men talking. What if more decided to go back? What if the Kylers did? What would I do? I had to get west to Oregon country. I *had* to.

The next morning, when we were ready to set out, Mr. Silas began by announcing that he wanted to leave an hour earlier every day. Andrew Kyler spoke up. "If you don't allow time for the horses to graze, we'll start losing animals."

Mr. Silas looked at him. "Well, then, maybe it wasn't so smart to buy up every horse in every town you come through and herd 'em along."

I bit my lip. In one long day, we were suddenly a party of only eleven wagons. Eleven. All of the guides had said that any party fewer than twenty-five wagons was too small to be safe. Some said thirty or more.

It was also too small to avoid Grover. His family's wagon fell into place in front of the McMahons now. I saw him two or three times that morning, walking not far in front of me and the Mustang. I dropped back, stopping to let the Mustang graze when I could.

Midmorning, when Grover glanced around at a shout from his father, I did, too. I noticed a dark bruise on his face. Maybe he had been jolted to the floor of his wagon during the crossing. Maybe he had gotten into a fight with one of the other boys. Whatever the reason, he seemed distracted and downhearted. I wasn't glad, but I was relieved that he showed no interest in me or the Mustang.

Two nights later, the men had a meeting. They elected Mr. Kyler as their leader. I grazed the Mustang a little ways off and could hear them when they raised their voices. No one had really wanted Mr. Kyler. Mr. Silas wanted to run things and so did Mr. McMahon. Mr. McMahon wasn't tough or bold like Mr. Silas, but it was obvious that he was smart and that he had studied the guidebooks more than any of the rest of them.

Trouble was, some thought that Mr. Silas was tough and strong and that he'd get them to Oregon whether they liked him or not. Others thought he'd run the party straight into trouble. Some thought Mr. McMahon knew enough about the trail to make good decisions and wanted anyone *but* Mr. Silas in charge.

In the end, Mr. Kyler got elected because he was the only one enough of the men could agree on. He led the party south to miss some rough, rock-strewn country, and we found the Platte at low water again. Since the better grass was on the south side, we crossed back. Every evening the men hauled out their drawings and maps and consulted, usually ending up in shouting matches. It scared me. It scared us all. No one knew which way to go.

I looked at Mr. Kyler's maps more than once with Mrs. Kyler. No one can draw countryside with a few lines on paper. The lines didn't show dozens of little creeks and ravines and rocky flats that split the iron tire-rims and cracked the oxen's hooves. We did the best we could. We kept the Platte River more or less in sight and kept going.

One afternoon, we saw dot-sized wagons on the horizon ahead of us. The word passed down the line like water down a steep ditch. The men stepped up the pace without Mr. Kyler saying a word. Mr. Silas got his short dinner break and we stopped later than usual for supper. Everyone was excited, full of hope. Maybe we could simply join another party and go on to Oregon with a real guide.

The next morning, I barely had time to graze the Mustang before we set off. Even Mr. Kyler popped his whip and kept his oxen walking as fast as ever an ox can walk. We were all watching the trail ahead, happiest when we could see the wagons as tiny dots on the horizon ahead of us.

Two days later, the men voted for Andrew, Mr. Kyler, and Mr. Silas to go ahead on horseback and meet up with the other party. The next night, they came galloping back with bad news.

There were only three wagons, and the people in them had a sadder story than ours. Their party had been hit by a fever. They had buried a lot of people, and those left had split up. Some had stopped to nurse their ill, others had turned back, a few had turned south, hoping to escape the fever in warmer weather. They were so low on men that a woman was running the party, Mr. Silas said, and then he spat. And they weren't families. They were circus people. He spat a second time.

As soon as I heard the men say *fever*, my heart shrank inside me, and all the other news dimmed. But before long the arguments seeped back into my ears. *Everyone* had an opinion.

"We don't want to be around people who have been through the fever," Mr. McMahon said. Mr. Craggett and his wife agreed. Everyone did, really, and I was relieved. I had seen a wild fever kill my family. Better than any of these people, I knew how awful it was.

I noticed Mr. Kyler glancing at me all evening long, gauging how close I had led the Mustang to the men, whether or not I could hear. No one besides the Kylers knew my story, and I was glad. I didn't want anyone asking me about the fever now.

"They say it's been nearly two weeks since the last case," Andrew Kyler nearly shouted, trying to quiet the rest of the men down. Then he continued on in a more normal voice. "I've heard a week or two is usually plenty long enough for it to be gone."

There was a murmur of agreement. I started to feel uneasy.

"How many wagons are they?"

"Three," Mr. Silas repeated. "But only four people. And they are carrying banners and boxes of costumes and what all I don't know."

Another wave of murmuring ran through the men. I realized that I'd followed the Mustang as he grazed, and we'd ended up close to the campfire; but no one seemed to notice except Mr. Kyler, and he didn't say anything. So I stayed within earshot and kept listening.

"The boss lady's name is Miss Liddy McKenna," Mr. Silas said, pronouncing it like it left a bad taste in his mouth. "She's got fancy horses and all manner of nonsense. I say we angle north and just go around them."

"Doesn't seem right," Mr. Kyler said. "You elected me, and I say we ask them to join us as far as Fort Laramie. After that, anyone who wants to can camp and wait for a better deal to come along."

"But they aren't decent people," Mr. Taylor said. "She is *Miss* Liddy McKenna. She's traveling with men who are unmarried. It ain't right or proper, and I don't want my girls seeing a setup like that."

"Nonetheless," Mr. Kyler said. "Three more wagons makes us safer and stronger. You can cut your own path at Fort Laramie. We all can."

"I don't like it," Mr. Silas said. "Maybe we'll just go on north alone."

There was an awkward silence. No one liked Mr. Silas. Even his own companions hung back during the talks, their eyes averted, rarely speaking. But no one wanted him to leave us, not even me. When things were rough, he pitched in, hard.

No one answered him. They all sipped their coffee and sat back. He finally got the message and stopped pretending he was fool enough to strike out alone. "We'll stick to Fort Laramie. After that, I don't know."

"I agree with Benton Kyler," Mr. Taylor said reluctantly. "More wagons is better for all of us. The fever ain't likely to come up again, and we can all just stay clear of them anyway, stay out of their camp."

The men looked away, gazing out at the horizons in all directions. No one said anything right off, and I knew the decision had been made. I led the Mustang off a little ways, then let him graze again. No one said anything more. The men stood a few minutes, then split up and walked back to their own wagons.

CHAPTER ELEVEN

❧ ❧ ❧

*The two-leggeds have joined another herd. There are
horses among them—more horses than people. The
two-leggeds are calm and quiet, and I am glad for that.*

The day we came up on Miss Liddy McKenna
and her three wagons, every woman on the
wagon train had on her best bonnet and her clean-
est skirt. The Kylers' granddaughters' faces had
been scrubbed and their bonnet strings were neatly
tied. Mrs. Taylor and Mrs. Craggett had on what
looked like Sunday-go-to-meeting clothes. The
women were bound and determined to show Miss
McKenna what decent women looked like.

I was curious about Miss McKenna, too, but
the first thing I noticed as we got closer was the

horses, and I couldn't look at anything else for a few minutes. I had never seen horses like the ones in Liddy McKenna's party.

Two had spots that looked like someone had splashed them with white paint. The third was the color of the Mustang, but with a white mane and tail and white stockings on its legs. It had the oddest conformation, tall and lanky. There was one bay mare as big as any plow horse I had ever seen— she had spats of long dark hair that covered her pasterns and her hooves.

I stood back, afraid of the fever in spite of what everyone had said. No one really got close, but they all stared, just like I did. And when I stopped staring at the horses, I saw that the people were as interesting as the stock.

There was one Negro man of slight build who was shouting orders at two of the other men as we got closer. They were arguing with him in a way that made it clear they didn't mind making each other angry. Then they all laughed at something one of them said.

One of the men had his long blond hair tied back from his face with a strip of rawhide. The other was the tallest man I had ever seen, with odd, big hands and feet.

Mr. Kyler pulled his wagon to a halt, and the others creaked to a stop behind him. I could hear people whispering, saw the couples leaning toward each other on their driver's benches to talk without being overheard. Julia and Polly had their heads together, standing out to one side to get a better look. Even Grover had his chin up, staring.

The argument between the two men went on even as Miss Liddy McKenna herself walked toward us and stood with her arms wide, like a woman welcoming relatives into her home. That was odd, but not nearly as odd as her attire. She was wearing men's trousers!

"I am Liddy McKenna," she said. Her voice was loud and musical. "We appreciate your letting us join you."

There was an automatic murmur of responses. Only Charles Kyler's tiny wife called out, "Pleased to meet you, Miss McKenna."

The other women harrumphed and glared at her, but she seemed not to notice. I looked back toward Miss Liddy McKenna in time to see her bow from the waist, then straighten. "We are very grateful. We will endeavor to stay apart. I know you are all afraid of the fever. Any sensible person is."

She paused, waiting for anyone to answer. Mr. Kyler finally cleared his throat and spoke up. "We're glad to have the extra hands in case of need," he said. "Our plan is to get as far as Fort Laramie and figure out, each one of us, what is best from there. All are going to Oregon, if possible."

Liddy McKenna smiled at him, a smile so wide that all her teeth showed. There was another little rumble of disapproval from the women when she stepped forward and pulled off her hat, letting long, unpinned, reddish hair fall down her back. "We aren't at all sure where we are going yet," she told Mr. Kyler, loudly enough for all to hear.

There was a stunned silence in response to that announcement.

"We travel," she added. "We aren't looking to settle down."

No one seemed to know what to say to that, either. So the men just shouted back and forth with her for a while, arranging that her wagons would follow ours for the rest of the day and that we would make separate camps, but close together.

I led the Mustang off to the side, as always, when we got started up again, the drivers of our wagons pulling their teams in a wide arc around Liddy McKenna's wagons to take their place in the lead.

As I got closer to her wagons, I tried not to stare, but it was impossible. She noticed the Mustang and turned to meet my eyes.

"Beautiful horse!" she called.

I nodded, unable to think of a single thing to say.

"Is he fast?"

I shrugged. "I've never ridden him," I managed to call back to her. "No one has."

"Not even your pa?"

"I'm an orphan," I told her, calling it out loud enough for everyone to hear. Then I blushed hot enough to sear peaches for cobbler. I fell silent, amazed at myself.

She tipped her head and smiled. "Lost my folks, too, when I was nine."

That caught me off guard. "I was six," I said more quietly. We were passing her now, and I had to turn to hear her answer. She cupped her hands around her mouth to make sure.

"Later on, when the fever scare is over, you and I should talk."

I nodded, then faced front to follow the Kylers' wagon. I could feel Mrs. Craggett's outraged glare behind me and I knew that Mrs. Kyler would give me a talking-to first chance she got. But, somehow, I wasn't worried about being in trouble. I couldn't wait to get to know Liddy McKenna. Whatever else she was, she wasn't afraid of anything—or so it seemed to me that day. The idea fascinated me. It seemed like I spent most of my time afraid of one thing or another.

I looked back as the wagons swung up onto the rutted path again. Miss Liddy McKenna had her party organized and rolling a few minutes later, a hundred feet behind us. She was sitting astride the big, broad-backed mare with no saddle or bridle on it at all, leading the way.

"We can all hope that this hasn't been a terrible mistake," Mrs. Craggett said, loudly enough for the Kylers and me to hear.

"She's had to make her way," Mrs. Kyler called back over her shoulder. "Some have to do that."

I smiled, pleased as a cat with cream over the

way Mrs. Kyler had taken Miss Liddy's side, at least a little.

The next day was hot, and the dust hung in the air around us. No one talked much. The days were all getting hot, and it was worse and worse for traveling. The grass was thinning, and we saw more and more of the silvery gray-green of sagebrush on all sides. It was dry—so dry that our lips cracked and split. My lower lip got a bloody fissure that wouldn't heal. The Mustang often sniffed at it, like it worried him.

If it had not been for the Platte River on our left-hand side most days, we could not have made it so far in such heat. We crossed it again in search of better grass. It was a puny thing now, half as wide as it had been. Then, as we went along, the trail drew farther and farther from the shallow river.

We found springs sometimes, to refill our water barrels—and the water wasn't as muddy as the river water. But it wasn't always good water. Often it had a terrible, bitter taste that made my mouth pucker. Sometimes the Mustang wouldn't drink it at all, and, though he seemed all right, I worried about him. He was losing weight. I could feel his ribs when I patted him with the flat of my hand.

In the middle of one long and miserable afternoon, we came to a place where the land suddenly dropped down into a hill so steep Mr. Kyler pulled his oxen to a halt and stared at it. I led the Mustang closer. There were wagon ruts in the soil as far as I could see. That meant others had come this way, so it had to be possible. It didn't *look* possible, though—it was that steep. I could see trees at the bottom. Trees! That meant shade and probably a creek or a spring.

Mr. Kyler handed the reins to Mrs. Kyler and set the wagon brake, then he climbed down off the driver's bench. The oxen lowered their heads and closed their eyes, grateful, as always, for every possible second of rest they were given.

The menfolk gathered, squinting in the sun, standing in a group at the top of the hill. "That's steeper than the Council Bluff Road," Mr. Kyler said. Everyone else just nodded. They could see that much for themselves.

"We go one at a time," Mr. Silas said. "If a wagon wrecks, there is no point in having others close to get in trouble."

"No one is going to wreck," Mr. Kyler said firmly. "But I am always in favor of a good precaution." He met each man's eyes for a few seconds. "One at a time, and every man lends his weight on a brake line for the rest."

They all nodded again, but I saw Mr. Silas scowling. I knew why. It was hot, the air shimmering close to the ground. There were fourteen wagons, counting Miss McKenna's. It was going to take the rest of the day, at least, and a lot of walking back up that terrible hill to help with the next wagon. Mr. Kyler wasn't paying attention to Mr. Silas's reaction. He was asking each man what he had in the way of stout rope.

It took every second of the livelong day, and everyone was exhausted by the time all the wagons were down the hill. The last long stretch was rock ledges and some of the wagons had to be unloaded and *lifted* down, inch by inch, ten men on each side, straining and sweating. I walked the Mustang down, glad I didn't have to perch on a slanting driver's bench, staring down that terrible hill.

Miss Liddy McKenna came last. She had refused Mr. Kyler's help—since no one wanted to go near her party anyway—and had astonished everyone by putting a heavy, odd-looking harness on the huge dark mare.

First, Miss Liddy ran a heavy rope from the harness to the rear axel of the wagon. Then the Negro man drove the two pairs of oxen while Miss Liddy sat backward on the bench, calling out commands to the big mare that followed.

"Hold up, girl!" she'd shout, and the mare would slow, the rope going taut as the weight of the wagon caught. Then Miss Liddy leaned forward again, "Ease up, pretty girl, ease up slow!" And every time, the mare would take tiny steps forward, as though she was tiptoeing, letting the wagon roll—but no faster than the oxen could walk. It was amazing to watch.

"You're that smart," I told the Mustang, then blushed, hoping no one had heard me. I glanced around. No one had; they were watching, as astounded as I was.

The men broke into a cheer as Miss Liddy's last wagon rolled onto the flat ground at the base of the hill. Their wives and daughters smiled tightly, then turned to their chores. All but Mrs. Kyler. She was grinning.

We made camp in that hollow. There was a spring with ice-cold, sweet water, a little creek deep enough for the boys to swim in. The sound of the water splashing lifted every heart, and the shade of the ash trees was a pleasure beyond words. There was an old cabin, a little thing, half rotting, that stood near the creek. I couldn't help but wonder who had built it. When I asked Mr. Kyler, he only shrugged his shoulders.

"Fur trappers. That's what people say. So far as I know Indians don't build log cabins, so it had to be trappers, French or English, back when the fur trade was booming in the twenties, I suspect. I'm sure Lewis and Clark didn't come this far south forty-three years ago."

Lewis and Clark—I had heard their names from my pa. I knew they had something to do with opening the western country, exploring it... but *forty-three* years ago? I drew a breath to ask more questions, but Mr. Kyler was patting my head, walking past me on his way to his next chore.

I lay awake that night, thinking about the trappers and the men who went with Lewis and Clark. How could they travel without a guide, without wagon ruts showing the way at least some of the time? They must have had a lot of help from the Indian people who knew the country, or they would all have taken bad routes on these endless plains and died of thirst.

As late as I went to sleep, I was still the first one up the next morning. I rose, shivering, and dressed, then checked on the Mustang. He was grazing quietly, so I stood at the edge of the creek, listening to the sound of that cool sweet water.

I wondered how Hiram was—and poor Annie. I said a little prayer that her hands would heal, that she wouldn't be crippled.

When a sound I didn't recognize startled me, I turned. There was nothing but rock and water and trees. I tilted my head, trying to hear past the pattering of the water, and I caught the sound again. Someone crying?

I walked closer, imagining one of the Kyler girls upset over some argument, or one of the Taylor girls, maybe the pale one. I tried to recall her name and couldn't at first. I rarely saw her at all; she was almost always in the wagon. Mary. Her name was Mary.

I am not sure what I intended to say or do, but it seemed wrong to ignore someone's tears, so I rounded the rocky outcropping on the south side of the spring and walked into the trees. Then I stumbled to a halt, blushing, wishing I had minded my own business. It was Grover, bent double, and when he raised his face I saw another dark, hard-lump bruise.

He glared at me. "Go away."

"I'm sorry," I said.

The look in his eyes was awful, desperate. "Get away from me!" he whispered, turning.

"I thought it was Mary crying or—" I stopped. "I'm sorry."

Without turning, he lifted one arm in a violent, angry gesture, like he was shoving at me. I spun around and ran back through the trees.

CHAPTER TWELVE

❧ ❧ ❧

*The sweet water and shade were good. I would
not have moved on until the weather cooled
at summer's end. But the two-leggeds did. Good
country or bad, they always move on.*

*W*e stayed another full day at the bottom of
that terrible hill. The Mustang was fidgety,
shaking his mane, high spirited in the dawn chill
when I led him out to graze. In the hot afternoon,
he dozed with the mares and the other horses in
the shade of the cottonwoods.

It seemed like Grover was avoiding me as much
as I was avoiding him from that day forward. I was
still afraid of him, but I understood him better,
too—all the bruises made sense, and his anger. I
remembered very clearly how I'd felt every time

Mrs. Stevens had given me a willow switching—I was sad, but I was furious, too. More than that—I had hated her for it. I couldn't *imagine* feeling that way about my own father.

I knew that Mr. Kyler and the other men wouldn't approve of Mr. Heldon beating his son, but, if they had noticed, they hadn't done anything to interfere. They wouldn't. No one would ever question a father's punishment of his own children.

On the day we resumed our journey, I caught a quick glimpse of Grover as he took his place behind his parents' wagon, then my view was blocked by the Taylors as they brought their wagon around to get into line.

For a time, the trail seemed like it was just plain strewn with wonders. Two days later, traveling through dry country dotted with sagebrush and only sparse grass, we spotted two rock formations that Mr. Taylor told us were named Courthouse Rock and Jailhouse Rock. Two days after that, we were close enough to see why. They really did look like grand buildings jutting into the sky, especially in the hot, shimmery afternoon. The Mustang stood close beside me as I stared.

Two days later we spotted an even stranger rock. Mr. Kyler called it Chimney Rock, and that's exactly what it looked like—if the house was a hundred stories tall. It was so odd. Out of that flat, dry plain there rose a hulking, rounded mound of rock; then, on top of that, a sloping cone shape; then, on top of that, connected to and hewn from the same stone, there was a thin spire that stretched high enough to pierce a cloud's belly.

Everyone stopped and stared. If it hadn't been so hot, I think some would have walked a mile or two closer for a better look at it.

After that, we passed most of a week without being astonished at anything, our days timed to the soft thudding of ox hooves. The Mustang drank water from our barrels; he had to, there was nothing else to drink.

Andrew Kyler fussed constantly over his stock. He had seven water barrels, which burdened his oxen with extra weight. The water was rationed out, the horses allowed only short drinks to make it last. Some of his horses looked pretty bad, their ribs jutting out, their hipbones knobby beneath their skin. Delia and Midnight looked better than most of the others—I tried to include them in the Mustang's dawn-dusk grazing at least sometimes.

One morning we came over a little rise and saw rock bluffs jutting up out of the ground, high and ragged. It took some time, but we found a rutted track that led around them, and the wagons creaked and groaned over the rough ground. The rock was sharp, and a lot of us put on shoes for the first time in weeks.

The Mustang and I got pretty far out in front as the oxen picked their way over the stony ground. He bent his head like an oversized puppy, sniffing at my shod feet while we waited for the oxen to plod their way up to us.

By the time we spotted Fort Laramie, the menfolk had been talking about it for days. They made it sound like heaven on earth. It didn't look like it to me. Still, the log stockade stood straight and the square towers on either end gave it a look of solid safety, at least from the far side of the Laramie River. I could see men moving around outside the big fences, and there was a circle of wagons farther up the little valley.

The stock drank their fill, and we waited an

hour or two so none would colic trying to swim with full bellies. Then we finally started across. Oxen bawled and balked at the water and refused to go forward.

Andrew Kyler rode a horse across, and we found out why. The river was only four or five feet deep, but it was so swift that water washed the horse sideways as it swam. With Andrew clinging to the saddle, it scrambled up the far bank a long ways downstream. I watched, along with everyone else, with a heavy heart. The Laramie River would not be an easy crossing.

The men set to work, walking up and down the banks, looking for a shallower place to cross. No one wanted to lose wagons in the current, of course, but no one wanted to run out of daylight before all were safely across either. Or most, I should say. Not all.

Mr. Silas wanted to go alone, and first, and he did just that. Before anyone could say a word about it, he ran back to his wagon and turned his team toward the crossing. "It ain't that wide or that deep," he shouted, then cracked his wagon whip.

"Hold up!" Mr. Kyler yelled at him. "Let us get a rope across and anchored first!"

But Mr. Silas either didn't hear or didn't care. His companions knew better than to argue with him, I guess, because we didn't hear a one of them speak up as the wagon rolled down the bank and into the river. One shared the driver's seat—I saw him grab at the bench. The ones in back clung to the wagon rails.

I reached up to touch the Mustang's cheek with the flat of my hand, afraid to watch but unable to look away. Mr. Silas's wagon team began to swim halfway across, and the wagon rose like a clumsy boat, angling downstream, dragging the team with it. Mr. Silas cracked the whip and shouted like a man gone mad, and, a few terrifying moments later, the team found its footing and the wagon swung around. It tilted dangerously, then righted itself as they staggered out and pulled it up the steep bank.

No one cheered. No one said a word. Mr. Silas had done something foolish and had gotten away with it. He whooped and stood on the footrest and stuck one fist into the air. Then he whipped up his team and started up the bank toward the fort. We all watched wistfully.

"Let's get to work," Mr. Kyler called. That seemed

to break the spell, and we all started the long round of chores we had become used to. The women packed everything tight, tied everything down, caulked the wagon beds; while the oldest Taylor boy fastened a rope to a tree on our side, swam the rope across the river and tied it to a stout tree on the other side. If anyone was washed downstream, they would have a chance of grabbing the rope.

The crossing seemed to go even slower than usual as we waited our turns. I knew without anyone telling me that it was too deep and too swift to wade, and I walked the Mustang down to Andrew's herd.

The Mustang whinnied, and the mares answered him. I turned him loose, and he took his place beside Delia and Midnight. I walked slowly back to the Kylers wagon, scuffing my feet. I hated leaving the Mustang.

The crossing was worse than usual. I clenched Mrs. Kyler's hand and I could see her lips moving when the wagon started to slew sideward, the wheels no longer touching the bottom. I knew she was praying. An eternity later, we felt the wagon jolt as the oxen touched bottom and began to pull.

Finally, the wheels turned against the rocky river bottom, and the wagon wrenched and swayed toward the far bank. I could feel Mrs. Kyler trembling a little as the oxen pulled us out of the river, but she smiled at me. "There's one more behind us. Thank you," she said, looking upward toward the sky.

Andrew and Ralph Kyler brought the stock across, and the Mustang helped them herd the mares up the bank. There were no animals lost, and everyone felt fortunate as we set up our camp a quarter mile or so from a circle of wagons that was already there. Mr. Silas camped with us like nothing had happened. Miss Liddy and her wagons set up a small distance away.

There was only a little daylight left, and we set about spreading out the blankets and clothes that had gotten wet. At dusk, we heard the fort gates creaking closed and men calling to one another from inside. By bedtime, the camp was about as comfortable as we could make it. I stood with the Mustang for a long time, then left him with the mares to sleep.

The next morning, Mrs. Kyler woke me early. "Let's go see what they sell here. Benton gave me a little money. Folks say it's expensive, but I want to look around."

I sat up on my pallet and spotted the Mustang. "Five minutes," I told Mrs. Kyler. She nodded. I pulled on my clothes and ran to tell the Mustang I was going to the fort for a little while. He nuzzled my neck, and I could feel the warmth of his breath. I hugged him, hard, then stood back. "If they have apples, I'll bring you one if I can."

He shook his mane and dropped his head to graze.

"Do you want something to eat first?" Mrs. Kyler said when I walked back.

I was hungry. I was always hungry. But the idea of our usual rancid bacon, cooked or raw, made my stomach tighten that morning.

Mrs. Kyler laughed quietly. "I know. When you know there might be something better, what we have here doesn't make your mouth water much, does it?"

I smiled at her. We set out across the clearing in the dusky light. A few others were up, but barely. I could hear sleepy voices inside the wagons, but no one was stirring yet.

I looked over at Liddy McKenna's camp. No one was up there, either.

"If there is one bargain in the place, we'll find it," Mrs. Kyler whispered. I nodded and smiled, feeling silly and free, like we were off on a lark.

The fort's doors had been opened, and the young man standing beside them nodded as we went past. Then he yawned and stretched.

Inside the fence, the fort looked like a small town crammed into close quarters. There was a blacksmith's forge, the fire already glowing. There was a cooper's, with barrel staves stacked in bundles, waiting to be put together. There was a dry goods store—well, it was sort of like a store. It was more like a tent awning with goods on blankets beneath it.

And there was the fort trader's shop. We went inside, staring at the stacks of clothing, the grocery goods on shelves along the walls. I glanced around. The shelves held bags of salt and coffee. There were parcels of corn and peas and beans, too. Along one wall there were a few trunks, some bedsteads, and sundry other household goods set along the side.

It was obvious where most of the trader's stock

had come from. People going west all too often packed more than they needed and regretted the extra weight. We had seen chairs and beds left to rot on the plains. As thin as some people's oxen were wearing already, I knew we would see more as we went.

"What do you pay, sir?" Mrs. Kyler asked the clerk, obviously thinking along the same lines. "I have a washtub that's too small for my needs and some window curtains that are just in my way."

"I pay well enough for anything I don't have," the man said, stepping out from behind a wooden counter. "Trouble is, I have just about everything."

Mrs. Kyler looked at him. "Is that so?" She put her hand on my shoulder and leaned down to whisper in my ear. "Go look around a little. See what he has for sale."

I nodded and glanced back out the open door toward the tall stockade gates. More people were trickling in. It wouldn't be long before our whole party was inside the fort—and probably everyone from the other camp, too.

The doorway darkened, and a man came in. He caught the clerk's eye. "Where are the letters?"

I watched the clerk point. "There's a half barrel on the back wall."

I caught my breath. *Letters?* I hadn't even *thought* about the fort being a post office, but it made sense. My heart was racing. If my uncle Jack had answered me...the letter could be here. I glanced at Mrs. Kyler. She was watching me. She smiled and nodded.

"Which one is the letter barrel?" the man asked from behind me. The shop owner gestured with his chin. "Right over there."

I saw it. Someone had cut a pickle barrel in half and set it up on a crate. The man was closer, and I had to keep myself from running across the hard dirt floor.

I watched, barely breathing, as he went through the soiled letters. When he had handled each one twice, he made a sound of disgust and turned to leave. I guess he could see my hopes on my face, because he nodded at me as he passed. "I wish you better luck than mine," he said kindly.

I stared at the barrel and swallowed hard as I walked toward it. It was hard for me to reach inside, but I took out every single letter, then went through them slowly, reading each person's name, the name of each town and territory or state.

A few of the letters had street numbers—people in big cities numbered their houses, I knew. Most of the packets just had names and towns and sometimes directions. "Mr. Earl Franklin's place, three miles north of Mad Creek Village, Kansas Territory," one said.

My heart was fluttering like a bird against my ribs. I stared at each letter, read every word of the address, then dropped it back into the barrel. Then I would hold my breath and allow my gaze to fall on the next one.

I was halfway through the stack when I felt my heart's fluttering stop an instant, then begin again. I stared at the letter in my hand. It wasn't for me. It was *from* me. Jack Rose, it said, in my own handwriting. *Jack Rose and family, Oregon City, Oregon Country.* The paper I had folded over the letter was still tied securely with the cotton twine I had used more than a year before. There were stains all over the paper, but the writing was still very clear. So was the message someone had scrawled across the top of the packet.

"*NEVER HEARD OF HIM.*"

I felt sick, then I gulped in a long breath, laid the letter to one side, and forced myself to finish going through the stack. When I had, I turned around. "This one is mine," I told the man in the apron. He nodded without looking up from his work. I shoved the letter inside my bodice.

It didn't mean anything, I told myself, trying not to cry. And I knew it was true. One returned letter didn't mean anything at all. I had written several letters, and just because one person in Oregon City hadn't known my uncle Jack, that didn't mean he wasn't there. I looked around the shop. Mrs. Kyler had left.

I walked outside and stood near the fort trader's door and pulled in one deep breath after another, looking for her. I was sure Uncle Jack would answer me. He was my mother's only brother, and she had been his only sister.

He had written my mother twice, and he would write me. It was too bad his answer hadn't gotten to Iowa while I was still there, but it didn't matter. I knew what it would say. Uncle Jack would tell me to come west to Oregon, that I could live with him and his wife and their children, that I would be welcome. Of course. Of course he would say that. What else would he say?

I stood up straighter. Maybe Uncle Jack's answer was sitting on Mrs. Stevens's old porch right now, brought by some neighbor who had gone into town. The McCartys wouldn't read it, I was sure. They would send it back to him. Maybe in a year, when I had been living with my family in Oregon for months, Uncle Jack's letter would come back, carried by farmers and stage coaches and people in wagons like the Kylers. We would read it together and laugh to think that the letter had traveled the Oregon trail *twice* to find me.

"Katie? Katie!"

I looked up, startled. It was Mrs. Kyler, looking flustered. "Benton sent Polly to bring us back. He says the other camp has a guide, and the man is coming to talk to us. I want to hear what he has to say."

I nodded, my thoughts still with the letter inside my bodice. I didn't need to read it. I knew exactly what it said. I had been so unhappy, so desperate when I had written it.

"Katie?"

I looked up at her.

"Did you hear me?"

I nodded, and we began walking. Polly had gone ahead, I could see her running across the grassland, framed by the big stockade doors, her dress flying out behind her.

Mrs. Kyler put her arm around me. "No letter?"

I shook my head. I didn't want to explain.

"I'm sorry," she said. She held me close to her side for a moment, then let me go. "It will all work out for you, Katie," she whispered.

Neither of us said another word as we walked. I could smell cook fires and bacon as we neared our camp, and it made my mouth water. She looked into my face and smiled. "Bacon sounds good now, doesn't it?"

I nodded, and we both laughed.

"Back to work, I guess?" she asked. I tried to smile at her. She patted my head. "Will you get the fire made? I'd love to eat before the wagon guide gets here."

I nodded again.

She tilted her head. "Are you all right?"

"Yes," I told her. And it was true. I was all right.

I was fine. We would soon be on our way—maybe with this new guide to show us the shortest, easiest trail to Oregon. Uncle Jack was there. One of my letters had just gotten lost, that's all. Just one.

The sun was up and warm against my skin as I raked back the ashes. I crumpled the letter and used it to raise a flame, then added kindling wood. I knew exactly what the letter said and it didn't matter anymore. I didn't need to tell my uncle I was living with Mr. and Mrs. Stevens now, working too hard and eating too little, scolded and switched all the livelong day. Things had changed. I had saved myself from them, and I would get myself to Oregon, too.

Once the fire was crackling, I ran to check on the Mustang. I told him about the letter, and he nuzzled me, nibbling at my hair and cheek as I talked. I hugged him and patted Delia and Midnight, then told them all I had to go back to help Mrs. Kyler.

She was bending over the fire when I got there, the bacon sizzling and the coffee on. Breakfast was almost ready. Carrying firewood for her, I began to hum a tune. I had no idea where it had come from at first, then I remembered. It was a song my mother had sung, an old one, from Ireland, from her grandmother.

I tried to remember the words and couldn't, and it made me sad until I realized that Uncle Jack must know it. Even if I couldn't remember it, he would be able to teach it to me. The thought made me smile. This long journey wasn't taking me somewhere strange and scary. It was taking me *home*.